Cook's Bones

BOBBI MILLER

ISBN 978-1501063367

DEDICATION

For Brian,

who encouraged me to write;

and for John,

my partner in crime

February 11, 1779 - Kealakekua Bay, Hawai'i

Kelani stood barefoot on the beautiful shores of Hawai'i, her hand pressed against her forehead shading her big brown eyes from the bright midday sun. Turquoise water lapped against the black lava surrounding her feet, but the rhythmic ripples failed to sooth her like they usually did. A foreboding tattoo hammered against her ribs as she watched the enormous ship heave to, its split foremast in danger of breaking in two and plunging into the sea. The wicked storms must have damaged it, forcing the ship to return to the calm waters of Kealakekua Bay for repair.

Captain James Cook, the great Chief of the Englishmen, had returned after departing just a week ago amid increasing unrest.

When his ship, with its billowing white sails, arrived the first time, her people thought he was an ancestor returned from the heavens. The villagers soon realized, however, that the Englishmen were very much flesh and blood, just as the villagers were, possessing not a saintly aura, but rather a lust for life, with the same physical urges for food, water, and women. This time their arrival bespoke danger, especially since the men in her village had become greedy, coveting objects from The Englishman's fascinating material world.

Kelani feared Cook's return would end in a deadly clash. She feared his return would demand the greatest sacrifice any island people could offer. She feared the villagers' blood would spill like water over a cliff. In vast quantities.

Ignoring the feeling of uneasiness, suddenly distracted by a rumble in her stomach, she deserted her favorite spot along the water's edge in search of food. Yet she could not shake the cloak of impending doom that had shrouded her. As she crouched behind one of the village's many ancient lava stone walls, plucking succulent fruit from the small banana tree, voices floated over the barrier. She tried not to eavesdrop, but it was hopeless. So she moved in closer and listened as the village men spoke in low tones about stealing and stripping one of the great English Chief's smaller vessels under the cover of darkness. They wanted the nails and iron pieces embedded in the vessel, items which couldn't be produced here on the island. Kelani knew from experience that Captain Cook and his men, like all sailors at sea, must remain self-sustaining because the loss of even one small boat could mean the difference between survival and perishing at sea when they set sail again. Two years ago, her father's small fleet of canoes had been attacked by men from the neighboring island of Maui. Her father and his crew were able to fend off the attack, but they lost their food and water in the melee. To escape, they were forced to paddle far out into the sea. Twenty-three days later, her father's lifeless body returned to land, carried by his surviving, emaciated, exhausted crew. So Kelani, like so many women whose men went out to sea, knew first hand of the hardships and dangers the vast ocean wielded on its trespassers.

She also knew the theft the men were planning would be interpreted as an aggressive attack. How could it not?

Later that afternoon, the glow of the setting sun created long shadows of the sails as the English warship anchored again in Kealakekua Bay. Soon afterward, the Englishmen wanted food, as well as more logs to cut into planks, spars and masts for repairs to their vessel. When Cook's ships had anchored in Kealakekua Bay before, the chiefs and priests had ordered the villagers to be generous with their offerings of supplies, but as a result, although no one in the village went hungry, this time Kelani knew there was no extra food to spare for the Englishmen. The recent hikes into the hardwood forests, and the hard labor required to cut and haul logs back to the bay, had sapped the strength of most of the able-bodied village men. Dissention had risen amongst the villagers, which they aimed at the Englishmen, but also at the chiefs and priests, for the first time since Kelani could remember, although nothing had come of it then.

Now, nearly a week after Kelani had overheard the village men speak of thievery, she watched the English Chief, Captain Cook, row ashore with a small group of men he called 'marines'. The impending doom she could not shake still encompassed her like dense fog. Kelani knew this time the result of the dissention amongst the villagers would end differently. She could feel it in her gut.

She scurried to her secret vantage point on the cliff above the village, danger as palpable as the rough stones under her bare feet. When Cook stepped from the small boat, his voice echoed across the bay as he shouted and shook his fist toward the sky. From her position above the beach it was obvious he was furious about something. Did that mean the village men *had* stolen his vessel as they had threatened to do?

With a sinking heart, she watched her brother lead the way as her people crowded the bay, their anger rising to match Cook's. As the village men raised their voices to shout above Cook's, they shoved the village chief aside.

Then Kelani's brother hurled the first stone.

Horrified, Kelani watched the black lava stone arc through the heady tropical air before it struck one of the marines on the head. He staggered. A trickle of blood oozed from his chin.

The mob howled. Evidence of blood reinforced the new knowledge that the Englishmen were mere mortals. The village men reached into the tall grasses near the shore, grabbing spears and clubs that they must have placed there in anticipation of an altercation. Others snatched stones. Suddenly a full-fledged assault ignited against the Englishmen.

Loud bangs echoed off the lava cliffs jutting from the bay.

Several of the village men fell to the water, even though they were not close enough to have been stabbed or clubbed. Kelani knew the sharp report from the long tubes held by the marines had to be responsible, but how? How did loud sounds kill her people?

Rather than intimidate or scare, the loud bangs and the fallen men further incited the mob of villagers. The village chief and priests suddenly disappeared, so the situation quickly escalated out of control. Stones flew through the air, many of them striking the Englishmen with deadly precision.

Cook and his men must have quickly realized they were in a dire situation. They must have decided it was time to move out into deep water, out of reach of the flying lava stone missiles. From Kelani's vantage point, it appeared that the boat's oarsmen struggled against the powerful foaming waves, rowing with desperation to help the marines maneuver the long boat around. Yet Cook remained standing in knee-deep water, facing his attackers, brandishing his gleaming long knife, his sword, as the Englishmen called it. Kelani watched in awe of Cook's bravery, but she knew he would perish if he didn't retreat with his men.

Finally, with the long boat repositioned, several marines shouted for Cook as they clambered into the boat. Cook turned and began to rush through the water toward his men. But the swell of the waves prevented swift movement and the mob of village men howled in victorious anticipation while surging forward from the shore into the shallow water.

Kelani's hand flew across her gaping lips as someone clubbed Cook hard enough to cause his back to arch, halting his forward momentum. Yet Cook remained standing until another villager stabbed him in the shoulder with an iron dagger stolen from the Englishmen's ship.

The great Chief of the Englishmen plunged face forward into the frothing surf.

Two villagers rushed forward. For a moment, Kelani thought they intended on aiding Cook. Instead, they held Cook's head under water. Others rushed to join in, stabbing and clubbing Cook over and over. Once again, the long noisy tubes the marines were using made more loud banging noises, but Kelani remained focused on Cook's demise, until she noticed several other lifeless bodies floating on the waves in the shallow waters. Villagers slain by Cook's marines. Four uniformed bodies also floated face down. Kelani felt numb.

The marines in the long boat began a frenzied rowing motion, away from the shore toward their ship, leaving their dead mates in the bloodstained waters lapping the shores of Kealakekua Bay.

Kelani's body quaked. A fear deeper than the sea engulfed her. The slayings would incite the gods. And there would be no escape from their wrath.

Terrible things would happen because of the wild impulses and frenzied behavior of her people.

The visit from Cook had been their chance to learn from a great civilization. Kelani was fascinated with the possibilities a new world might introduce, but moments ago the opportunity evaporated before her eyes as she crouched on the ground, hidden by the fragrant Hibiscus bushes encompassing her vantage point. The heady fragrance that she usually loved almost made her sick.

The villagers fished lifeless bodies from the water, sorting the Englishmen from the Hawaiians. They carried the Englishmen into the hills, leaving the villagers behind for their families to claim. Heavy sadness crushed Kelani. The deaths were momentous.

The great Chief of the Englishmen carried King Kalani'opu'u's name and the King carried Cook's Hawaiian name, Kuki. Their identities had been intertwined in a ceremony during Cook's first visit to the island. So when Cook died, King Kalani'opu'u's kapu was broken. The King's status as ruler was now in jeopardy.

Kelani knew what would happen next.

And it would be barbaric.

Darting barefoot along the hillside, Kelani remained hidden in the dense vegetation. When she arrived at her destination, she knelt behind a banana tree, her graceful hands parting the large fan-like leaves providing camouflage from the mortuary site above Ka'awaloa. A fire pit had already been stoked to the beginning stages of a bonfire. Heat penetrated the dense foliage, warming her bare shoulders. Frenzied chanting spewed from the mouths of the priests. She forced herself to observe the rituals. It would be heinous and hideous. Yet she must watch. She had to know how ferocious the gods would be.

It was horrifying.

Despite her courage, she clamped her eyes shut as the half-crazed priests dismembered the great

Englishman and stripped the tissue from his bones. Then she watched the priests and lesser chiefs start their triumphant whirling and dancing as they held the great Englishman's bones in the air.

Suddenly, the acrid smell of burning flesh permeated the air. Kelani turned away, bile rising to her throat as one after another priest and chief consumed the seared flesh, a ritual that meant they now possessed the great Englishman's powers. She dared not utter a single sound, for if she were discovered, she too would be thrown into the raging bonfire.

Dawn finally broke as the priests and lesser chiefs began the ceremony of dividing the bones and wrapping them in bundles. Four runners were chosen to deliver the bundles of the marines' remains amongst various chiefs across the island. The great Englishman's remains, however, would be the property of King Kalani'opu'u, who remained entwined with Cook despite his death.

Kelani's brother, whose bravery in confronting the English was noted and honored by the priests, was singled out to deliver the bundle containing the great Englishman's remains, a task which he sprinted off to accomplish.

And unbeknownst to him, Kelani followed.

It had been a mistake to see what she'd seen. She was neither of royal blood, nor priestly castes. And she was a woman. This would hang like a curse over *her* head for eternity. It would damn her to a living hell. But she had no choice. She had to know.

The following evening, when Captain Cook's men demanded his remains be returned to their ship,

Kelani wondered how the chiefs would handle this, since King Kalaniʻopuʻu had taken Cook's bones into a cave in the cliff above Kealakekua Bay, accessible only by rope. She'd heard the King's grief was deeper than the ocean at the news of Cook's death. The allegiance and brotherhood he felt toward the great Chief of the Englishmen had been shattered by the violent deaths on the King's shores, and since the King had not yet returned to the village, no one knew how long he would remain in mourning.

So a priest swam out to the ship to tell the Englishmen they needed more time to recover Cook's remains.

Two days passed.

Then Kelani watched a much younger priest paddle out to the ships anchored offshore, carrying a piece of flesh from Cook's thigh as a sign of honor. She had no idea what transpired while the priest was onboard, but four days later, she watched the procession down the mountainside. Tears streamed down her cheeks as they presented the great Englishman's next-in-command with the bundle containing his remains, covered with a cloak of black and white feathers. Late in the afternoon, she wept as she watched Cook's wooden coffin slide over the rail of his flagship in what appeared to be some sort of military ceremony. The English flag flew at half-mast. Deep booms from the Englishmen's large guns echoed off the cliffs, as the weighted coffin sank into the deep blue waters of Kealakekua Bay.

The following morning, Kelani stood barefoot on the beach and watched King Kalaniʻopuʻu's son paddle out to the ship. She heard later that he had wept while onboard. It was a sentiment she fully understood.

Great sadness consumed her as she watched the ships unfurl their white cloud sails and disappear from Kealakekua Bay that evening, leaving the great Englishman's bones to decay in the briny depths of the sea.

That night, her brother, a man she trusted with all her being, told her the chiefs had given Cook's men the remains of a marine, all except for the hands. Cook's hand had a distinctive scar, so Cook's hands were substituted for the marine's hands to trick the Englishmen into thinking Cook's remains had been returned.

Kelani was horrified. This behavior would not please the gods.

*   *   *

On the first anniversary of Cook's death, Kelani made certain she was nowhere around when the chiefs paraded through the villages with Cook's bones. Her brother participated in the display of great power over her people. Kelani could not abide the spectacle.

Year after year, the great Englishman's bones were paraded through the villages. Year after year, disease and incessant warfare decimated her people, including her brother. The gods were angered, both by the deaths of the Englishman, and by the deceit over his remains.

This had to stop.

Kelani vowed to steal and hide Cook's bones herself one day. Someone had to appease the gods and bring peace and prosperity back to her people.

But the years passed. Missionaries arrived in 1819,

and with them came censure, the demise of the traditional Hawaiian ways, and the banishment of the ancient gods. Now an old woman, who had married and had children under the old gods, Kelani simply couldn't bring herself to convert to Christianity. She struggled with their declaration that there was only one God. How could only one God create the skies, the sands, the seas? But powerful changes had overtaken her people. If the Christian converts discovered the bones, they would destroy them, which would anger her ancient gods even more. And how much more death and destruction could her people endure?

Kelani never told her husband, or her children about the secret of the bones. Her husband had been killed in one of the incessant wars against neighboring regions and islands, and her children had succumbed, one by one, to accidents and disease. Kelani knew all her peoples' bad fortunes could be attributed to that fateful day on the beach of Kealakekua Bay all those years ago.

Despite her advancing age, and the challenges it would pose, Kelani decided to hide Cook's bones.

And so, Cook's bones disappeared.

Four years later, Kelani lay in a weakened state on the woven mat that served as her bed, fully aware she could not pass from this life into the next with her secret silenced forever. Her breathing labored as the weight of grief consumed her, shutting down her heart. Losing her beloved husband and children to the gods' wrath years earlier hadn't diminished her abiding and aching love for them. She was anxious to meet them in the afterlife. Yet even in this dark hour of waiting, she was not alone. Her cousin's daughter, Haili, visited her deathbed, and with all the strength she could muster, Kelani whispered in Haili's ear, imparting the wisdom and knowledge of her generation. Then, when she knew it was time, she drew enough air into her lungs to whisper the critical details about where she had hidden Cook's bones. Her life was not complete until her cousin's daughter understood the full importance of this revelation. With one last breath, she reiterated how crucial it was for Haili to pass this knowledge to each succeeding generation, but only to one person who would guard and revere the secret, lest the gods become angered yet again.

For Kelani, the impartation finally released her spirit. She took her last breath on earth and through the shining light she saw her beloved. She placed her hand in his when he drew her spirit toward him as the setting sun cast its rays across the beautiful turquoise waters lapping the shores of Kelani's Kealakekua Bay.

CHAPTER ONE

"Where to, bruddahs?" the cab driver asked, while heaving two ballistic nylon rolling bags into the trunk of the taxi parked curbside at the Honolulu International Airport.

"Take us to the corner of Onahau and Hibuscus Streets," Doyle said, raking his hand through thinning sandy hair as his keen gaze skittered across the arrival level of Honolulu Airport.

"No problem."

Doyle yanked open the rear door, and nodded to his companion. "Get in."

"I'll get in on the other side," Collins said, grasping the end of his charcoal bespoke Super 220 merino wool suit sleeve, pulling it down past the pale blue cuff of his shirt. His eyes narrowed. "That hideous cheap beige sports-jacket appears to have been slept in. You will never impress our clients looking like that."

"Bite me, Collins. Not everyone spends upwards of

five G's on a stupid suit. Now, get in."

Collins smirked as he sauntered around the taxi to the other side.

Fifteen minutes later, the taxi jerked to a halt in front of a 1920's three storey whitewashed building at the corner of Onahau and Hibiscus Streets. The Mom & Pop grocery store at street level boasted tattered posters that suggested indulgence in various sugary substances would satiate the appetite. A wave of repulsion swept over Collins. The faded wooden sign above the door announced "K. Ching Groceries and Sundries". The windows of the second and third floors had been papered with cheap prints of Chinese maidens, the once-bright colors washed and faded by ten thousand days of harsh tropical sunlight.

"Wait here. We'll be back in a couple minutes," Doyle said.

"I gotta keep da meter runnin, bruddah."

"Keep the meter running, but open the boot and wait for us," Collins said.

"Da boot?"

Doyle rolled his eyes. "The trunk. He means open the trunk." Then he glared at Collins. "You're not in jolly ole England, Collins. What the hell is the matter with you?"

Collins shook his head. "You American's should learn to speak proper English."

"And you Brits should learn to lighten up," Doyle said as he slammed the trunk shut.

Collins leaned through the front passenger window. "Wait for us," he said, assuming the taxi driver would watch as the grocer's dim doorway swallowed him and his irritating so-called partner.

Rows of sweet-smelling fruit tickled Collin's nose as they approached the butcher-block counter at the rear of the store. The elderly Chinese woman guarding the counter withered at the sight of them as if they had drugged her.

Without a word to either man, the woman slid off her stool and disappeared through the doorway behind her. Moments later a middle-aged Chinese man appeared in the same doorway and nodded to the men, waving them around the counter and through the door. He raised an upward palm toward wooden stairs ascending to the second floor and bowed.

"It smells like rotting onions in here," said Collins, yanking the silk hankie from his breast pocket to cover his twitching nostrils.

The second floor landing led to a single peeling green-lacquered door. Collins jerked his head toward the door. Doyle tested the cheap brass doorknob and when it gave way, they passed through without knocking.

The room ran the entire length of the second floor. As he tucked his hankie back in his breast pocket, Collins noticed the reverse images of the Chinese maidens on the sunlit prints covering the filthy windows. Three long folding tables, with high-density polyethylene plastic tops, scarred by years of enduring multiple cigarette burns, were situated in a U-shape along one end of the enormous room. The stagnant air and the stench of sweat and stale nicotine made Collins feel a tad faint. He glanced at Doyle. Doyle's broad face and stocky build showed no signs of discomfort. Nothing seemed to faze Doyle, Collins thought.

Sitting behind the tables were thirteen men, exhibiting distinctive Hawaiian features and long kinky hair flowing past their shoulders. *Not a man here is under 300 pounds*, thought Collins. They wore sweat-soaked bold-colored tank tops, exposing massive brown arms covered in traditional Polynesian tattoos, all with the exception of the biggest man in the group seated at the center of the middle table. His right arm boasted traditional tattoos, but his left arm had only one, on his bicep – a death's head with two crossed Hawaiian state flags and "HHF" tattooed beneath the flags in bold block letters.

Doyle and Collins ambled across the rough wood floor, stopping short of the tables. Their bags hit the floor with a thud. Collins felt nauseous. Beads of sweat formed on his upper lip. His expensive suit began to feel like an electric blanket set on high. He was getting too old for this.

"You look like you go-wan ta sumbuddy's funeral," said the Hawaiian with the death head tattoo. "Mebbe yu-ahs, eh?"

Collins and Doyle glanced at one another and then back to the big man. "My colleague, Mr. Collins, and I traveled a long way to help you. Don't taunt us. Show us the money and the weapons, and we'll disappear," Doyle said.

The Hawaiian glanced at his unsmiling tablemates before his lips curled in a nasty sneer, exposing a gold canine crown. "Sure, bruddah, buh firse we need to make id all clear whad you go-wan do. We wan da bones. Cook bones. We wan dem soon. So we give you haff da money now, haff when we get da bones. Undastan?"

"We understand completely, Alekanekelo," said the tall Englishman, sweat beading on his forehead now. "But let's not dally. Give us what we need so we can get to work."

"You bedda nod fail us, Collin. Da brudderhood of da Hawaiian Hereditary Fron will track you down and make you pay us back . . . slow and painful. God id?"

"Yeah, yeah," said Doyle. "You'll get your bones and someday you might even get your islands back to a sovereign state. Maybe even have a king to rule over all."

A cacophony of metal against wood echoed around the room as all thirteen Hawaiians shoved their chairs back and stood, arms crossed, menacing scowls etched across their weathered faces.

Collins held his hands up in surrender. "Gentleman, gentlemen." His wan smile felt false even to him. "Ignore his sarcasm. We are here to help you get the bones," said Collins, firing a visual dagger at Doyle.

"Aw ride!" exclaimed Alekanekelo. "Here's da money and da guns." He tipped his head to one side and two of the Hawaiians reached down beside their chairs and grasped identical black ballistic nylon rolling bags. Collins' and Doyle's decoy bags were filled with old shoes that Doyle had picked up at Goodwill because the Hawaiians thought entering the building without anything, then leaving with big heavy black nylon bags would look suspicious. Maybe he was right. Maybe he was just paranoid. Collins wasn't sure. Alekanekelo slammed a large black briefcase on the table and flipped it open, revealing a Berretta and a Smith and Wesson.

"Da AR-15 is in da udder bag," Alekanekelo said, jerking his head toward the black nylon bag nearest him.

At that point, Collins knew these men were serious about getting what they wanted. It would be dangerous if anyone entertained a double-cross. Even though he was a British ex-MI-6 agent, and Doyle was a retired CIA agent, they would have to be at the top their game to stay ahead of these guys in the coming days. For a fleeting moment, Collins wasn't sure about this job. They weren't as young as they used to be. Or as quick. It might cost him his life if they were unsuccessful. For a fleeting moment, Collins wavered.

Doyle grabbed a bag, so Collins followed suit, noting the bags were much heavier than the ones they brought in. Then Doyle snatched the briefcase from the table, and Collins followed him as he strode toward the door, leaving the bags they'd brought in with them setting on the floor where they had dropped them.

"Doan you wanna count da money?" asked Alekanekelo.

Doyle stopped and turned to face the Hawaiians, eyes narrowed. "If it's not all there, Alek, we'll find you. To coin a phrase, it will be a very slow painful death." Doyle spun around and he and Collins started down the stairs.

True to his word, the taxi remained at the curb with the engine running. Doyle banged his fist on the trunk, and the driver popped it open. They heaved the black nylon bags into the trunk and Doyle slammed it shut before he and Collins climbed back into the back seat again.

"Back to the airport," Doyle said as he slapped the back of the front seat with his open palm.

"Bruddah, you jus came from dere."

"We suddenly found out we have business on the Big Island," Doyle said, irritation oozing from his tone.

"I don't feel well," Collins said. "Must have picked up one of your disgusting American flu bugs on the airplane."

"You're not going weak on me, are you?" Doyle sneered. "Those guys will feed us to the sharks if we fail." Doyle glanced out the cab window toward the second floor of the building as the driver pulled away from the curb.

"Wha kinda business you bruddahs in?"

"Antiques," Doyle said. "Now shut up and do your damn job."

CHAPTER TWO

The chocolate brown bikini top and pale-yellow surf shorts provided little protection from the scorching Hawaiian sun searing Nicole Blake's bare skin. Although the ensemble complemented her deep blue eyes, the shorts didn't afford much coverage of the deep pale scar lining the inside of her left thigh, a scar that traveled just above the hem of the shorts all the way to her kneecap, reminding her of her mortality. But her petite five-foot-three-inch frame, and the delicate hands and feet she inherited from her mother, belied the physical strength she possessed.

With the intention of rowing across Kealakekua Bay to visit Captain Cook's Monument, sweat beaded on her brow as she strapped a yellow plastic kayak to the roof of the Dodge Avenger she'd picked up from the car rental agency just off the Kona Airport property. She found herself breathing a little harder by the time she'd finished strapping the kayak down. The humidity was oppressive. Thank goodness she'd tied her shoulder-length blonde hair into a ponytail before she'd left the airport, although as the sun licked her neck, she wondered which was more uncomfortable, hair or sun.

Driving down the winding road to Napoopoo Beach with the windows up, the air conditioner on full blast neutralized the heady fragrance of roadside pikake flowers as the terrain progressed down the hillside toward the sparkling blue water below. Nicole's unawareness that she had obliterated this favorite sensory experience emphasized her concentration on finding Cook's bones. Was it even possible? And how would she know the bones were Captain Cook's, even if she did find them?

Years ago, her parents had found Cook's bones in the cliffs above the monument. Perhaps whoever had supposedly stolen them from her parents had put them back there again, thinking they were appeasing some god. Nicole shook her head at that last thought. It seemed unlikely. If someone were to steal the bones, why would they put them back where her parents had initially found them? And in the intervening years since her parents' death, anything could have happened to Cook's bones, even if they *had* been put back where they once were. The only clue Nicole had to go on was what Gran had told her on her deathbed, which wasn't much. "*Go to the monument*," Gran had whispered in her final moments. That was all she had said. And that command had been haunting Nicole for a year. Now, the thought of dangling by a climbing rope for hours on end, searching a multitude of holes in a cliff for Cook's bones, seemed a little daunting and ambitious, until

21

she'd exhausted all other options. But the hours she'd spent on the Internet and in the local library had yielded zero information on the whereabouts of Cook's bones, so now it seemed more sensible to kayak across the turquoise waters of Kealakekua Bay to conduct a little hands-on research around the old village ruins where Cook had met his demise, even if it did mean she'd eventually end up dangling by a climbing rope near Cook's monument for hours on end searching the holes in the cliff side.

Was it plausible that someone had put the bones back in the same place? And if so, was it a trap? Her parents hadn't been the first casualties in the hunt for Cook's bones. Someone had kept them concealed and would continue to kill to ensure they stayed that way.

And if it was a trap, she'd be in dire straights.

Nicole came to the end of the road, which terminated in a T-intersection. To the right lay Napoopoo Beach, with a picnic shelter, a water catchment tank and a few parking spots. Across from the shelter was a large house built on lava rocks along the water's edge. To the left, the road led through a small community of ramshackle houses, then out along the coast. Straight ahead was a small parking area next to an old cement wharf. Nicole pointed the rental car straight, and parked it. On the cement wharf, where her kayak could be dropped in the water, her reflective state of mind was broken by a weathered middle-aged Hawaiian man, clad only in a pair of tattered black boardshorts, rushing toward her to offer his assistance. Against her better judgment, she agreed to let him help her, but only because it would be nice to have someone else muscle the awkward heavy object from the roof of the car.

"You paddle to da monumen before?" the man asked, sweat beading on his forehead as he worked.

"Yes, a few times. I'm interested in the history of Captain Cook."

The Hawaiian man leaned toward her, his hot, beer-laden breath fanning her face. "Ya know, da Hawaiians dint send any of Cook bones back to Englan," he whispered, his brown eyes darting from side to side as he spoke. Surprised at his declaration, Nicole raised an eyebrow and glanced around, too. "And my great-granmudder tell me where dey are," he continued to boast in raspy whispers, as if he were sharing an inside secret. "When I ged da buyer line up, I have moe money den da Pope."

Nicole frowned. Was this man clairvoyant? Had she mentioned that she was looking for Cook's bones? Was it emblazoned on her forehead? It seemed odd that he felt compelled to share this information with her at that moment. Unless he was simply trying to enrich the tourist experience in an effort to obtain a larger tip with his ironic tale. The latter seemed more likely, she decided, shaking her head while giving him a discouraging frown. If he spoke the truth, she knew boasting about it to the wrong person could cost him his life, but he seemed unaware of the risk, although sweat ran down his cheeks as if he were nervous. But the sun was hot, and he didn't appear to be tense, except for that furtive glance around the wharf before he spoke of his impending financial opportunity.

He pointed to a lawn chair setting in the back of a beat-up mud-covered tan pickup truck parked in the shade. "I be in dat same spod o'er dere when you ged back," he said with a toothy grin as he tucked his beefcake hand in the left front pocket of his grimy shorts for a moment.

If what he said was true, Nicole should take him up on his offer when she got back from her excursion and try to get some information out of him, although somehow she didn't think he'd wait around all day for her. The paunch dangling over the tattered black boardshorts suggested he'd more likely be long gone before sunset when she returned, sneaking Paco Loco or killing a six-pack while sizzling a hunk of Spam on the tip of a whittled Hala branch over an open fire.

The Hawaiian man dropped the kayak into the turquoise water with a gentle splash. Nicole averted her gaze to avoid a clear shot of his exposed butt-cleavage before stepping in the kayak, teetering as he held it in place while she sat down. Yet she was grateful for the Hawaiian man's assistance, butt-cleavage and all, for another reason. He might be a valuable resource, should she find herself in possession of a six-pack of beer and a case of Spam to offer as a bribe at some point in time. Nothing to what the Pope possessed, as was clearly this man's desire, but it might be enticing enough to mine more information out of this hard-working gentleman with the filthy drooping shorts.

Nicole smiled and handed the man a ten-dollar bill, emphasized her thanks with a wave of her left hand before shoving the kayak away from the cement and lava-stone wall with her paddle. She dangled her left hand in the warm turquoise water, then rotated her shoulders and rolled her neck counterclockwise before she began to paddle. As she moved away from the shore, she relished the effort it took to slice the water, dipping and pulling the paddle first on the left, then on the right, enjoying the rhythm of the sport. At the edge of her mind, though, she continued contemplating the Hawaiian man's declarations. More likely than not, he thought she was just another stupid haole female rowing across the bay in a single-seat kayak looking for romance, or adventure, or both. And all he probably wanted was her money, which suited her just fine since his idle chit-chat gave her something to think about other than her present situation. She hadn't intended on paying anyone to help her, but now she was grateful for the extravagance. Her training and experience at the Agency demanded much greater physical exertion than dropping a kayak a few feet over the side of a wharf, but as she continued the rhythmic paddling across the bay she decided to use the pseudo chivalry to her advantage, even though she would have to pay for it. Again, she weighed the Hawaiian man's comments about Cook's bones against the miniscule information her lengthy research had yielded. Had she not been rowing across to Captain Cook's monument she'd have thought the man's comments to be nothing other than alcohol, or cannabis-induced random boasting. But now, the more she thought about it, the more his declaration seemed plausible. Was it just a coincidence that he mentioned the bones to her? Perhaps today it was time to learn the truth.

As Nicole continued to paddle across the bay those thoughts continued to roll round and round in her head. The kayak bobbed on the swells as she paddled, her arms beginning to ache as the tide seemed to work against her. She glanced across the clear water toward the cliff, wondering if Cook's bones lay in one of those dark holes carved into the side of the steep cliff. The incredible beauty of her surroundings, the balmy tradewind on her face, the bright sunshine reflecting off the azure blue water, the sound of her paddles slapping a rhythm on the surf, were all lost on her as she attempted to concentrate on the constant rotation of her shoulders, the position of her hands on the paddle, the pull on her biceps with each stroke as she extended her legs and planted her feet on the foot rests. Then, finally, the dip, dip, dip of her paddle lulled her brain into neutral. She must clear her mind. She had to figure out what she wanted out of life now that everything had been stripped away.

What was her purpose for finding the bones?

What direction should she go?

How should she focus her efforts to obtain maximum results?

Not only was it time to discover the truth about the bones, it was time to discover her own truth.

A different rhythmic sound disrupted her reverie, her introspection, her meditation, assaulting her mind with its disturbance. Glancing over her shoulder, she realized another kayaker had been rowing across the deep clear blue water with increasing speed, slicing his paddle through the water like a competitor in an Outrigger canoe race. She heaved a sigh, displeased with the derailment of her thoughts, squinting against the blazing sun toward the cause of her annoyance.

Masculine. Muscular. Masterful.

Thick, light blonde hair, trimmed short around Eric North's face, segued into tousled sun-kissed tresses skimming the top of his bronzed shoulders in gentle curls. He was in dire need of a haircut. Dark sunglasses sat on the bridge of his Roman nose and hid the magnetic eyes she knew were lovely shades of amber and green, but they didn't hide the chiseled jaw line. A well-groomed mustache topped a sensual lower lip, tilted as if on the verge of laughter. She'd recognize that face anywhere. He'd kayaked around these islands enough to be considered an expert. Which meant only one thing. He was following her. And why he wore that standard-issue bright-orange life jacket, other than to emphasize the breadth of his shoulders and the muscular definition of his arms, was a mystery she was better off not solving. Shaking her head, she forced the thought to vacate her mind.

Until he slowed his pace to keep steady with hers. The thick powerful thighs were difficult to ignore.

Again she shook her head, this time with amusement. Why was he making such an effort to stay alongside her when he could easily glide right past and beat her to the monument? And now that he'd become aware of her visual inspection, she knew he wouldn't simply paddle by without social interaction. So she braced herself for the inquisition while staring straight ahead at Captain Cook's monument. Life would be so much easier if she could make her way there without listening to Eric's diatribe along the way.

"Well, well, well," he said in that deep melodic voice she knew too well, paddling alongside her, synchronizing his rhythmic strokes with hers, sun glistening on the silky pale hair of his forearms, dissolving any illusion she'd been entertaining about gaining the rocky shore in solitude. "Imagine finding you out here heading to Cook's monument." He shaded his eyes with his left hand and glanced around. "And all alone, too."

Heart pounding, a glare was all the response Nicole could muster. Thank goodness the deep expanse of dark blue water between them kept him from touching her with more than his glance and his mocking words. Ignoring him as best she could, she continued to paddle toward the shore.

When she increased her pace, so did he.

"Trying to ignore the shark in the water?" he asked, his sensual lower lip tilted with amusement, reminiscent of the first time she'd set ever eyes on him.

"I can do this without your help."

"I know that," his muscular arm swept through the air as he spoke, "but it's much more fun with a partner."

Convinced he was taunting her, she began vigorously paddling. Her shoulders and biceps began to burn. If she slowed a little, she might conserve some of her energy for the hunt, but at the moment all she could think of was putting as much distance between herself and her nemisis as possible. Laughter floated on the warm scented tradewind, burning her ears with its sarcasm as he allowed her to pull away from him. Awareness that he was mocking her spurred her on. This was her opportunity to prove she still had what it took.

Water swirled around the rocky shore as she approached. Her timing must be perfect. Riding a wave through a narrow passage of lava rock was the only way to make it without bottoming out and tipping over in the strong breakers. She waited, rowing backward, then forward a few strokes at a time, maintaining her position to take advantage of the next swell. As she approached, she bounced off a jutting rock, but managed to clear it as another wave swept in from the left on the approach through the jagged lava rocks. Once she made it through the narrow passage, she beached her kayak, pulling it up past the breakers to ensure it would remain there while she explored the monument, and the remains of the Hawaiian village that once thrived there.

Eric had either decided to leave her alone, or he'd beached his kayak further down the shore, laying in wait to assault her with his boyish charm as she approached the monument. Sure enough, as she hiked through the heavy-laden guava bushes, Kāhili ginger, banana and Hala trees, and Palapalai, Hāpu'u and 'Ehaha ferns that surrounded the village ruins, she spotted him waiting for her, dashing her hopes that she would be able to tackle the challenge of completing a mission on her own again. And this was a personal mission. She did not need help from another agent, least of all this man.

Navigating across a pebbled stream, she stopped and turned. "You just can't do it, can you?" she asked, her voice edged with annoyance.

"Do what?"

"Leave me alone."

"Why would you say that?"

"Because you're here." She threw up her hands in defeat. "You turn up everywhere. I'm trying to accomplish something on my own. You being here is more than coincidence." She turned away from him and continued to walk through the thick guava bushes toward the monument. When she stopped and turned again, he was arm's length away. "I don't need help, Eric."

That seductive grin hijacked his face again. His muscular chest, firm torso and Viking legs caused her heart to flutter, despite her effort to ignore his presence.

"But isn't it a lot more fun, now that we're doing this together? And by the way, what *are* we doing?"

She turned away, shaking her head. "I'm not even going to justify that remark with a response. You're too good at turning things to your advantage."

"As long as we both agree that I have the advantage."

"You know that's not what I meant."

"Hey, those were your words, not mine."

"And like I said, you take advantage of things."

"Such as?"

"I came out here to take care of some personal business and I don't need anyone's help."

"You're running away."

"I'm facing things head on."

"But you *are* running away."

"Don't start analyzing me. Please. I've had just about all of *that* I can take," she said.

Nicole dropped her yellow shorts, exposing the bottom half of her chocolate brown bikini. She perched on a smooth rock at the water's edge, donned a pair of blue flippers and shimmied a lime-green rubber mask down her forehead. With the snorkel tube dangling, she turned to face him again, catching the look of desire in his eyes as he took his time perusing her curvaceous bikini-clad body. "And put your eyes back in your head," she said as she slipped into the water. She bit the snorkel between her teeth to prevent herself from saying anything more. Let him ogle the back side of her if he wanted to. The water would distort the view.

His witty repartee hit a little too close to home. The discomfort associated with the guilt over the botched mission in Uganda, the deaths of three of her men, and the resulting forced leave-of-absence was almost unbearable. She unconsciously touched the long scar on her inner thigh, then withdrew her hand so Eric couldn't observe the gesture. She resented his joking. As a fellow agent, he knew her history, and it wasn't something to joke about.

It had cost lives.

As she propelled herself through the water, thrusting thoughts of Eric out of her mind, gazing down at the coral sloping down the steep bank of the ocean floor as shoals of brightly-colored Parrotfish in various sizes darted about, an epiphany flashed through her mind. Her redemption lay in recovering Cook's bones. Until she accomplished that, she could not rest. It would be her sign that she was ready to get back in the game.

In that moment, it became her promise. She'd made that promise to Gran a year ago, now she made it to herself. A promise she must keep so one day she might rest in peace.

A light brush across her ankle caused a reflex jerk of her head. Expecting to see a maybe a Kihikihi fish, she was annoyed to see Eric's hands near her flippers instead. She stopped swimming, popped her head above the surface and spat out her snorkel. When she stopped, he stopped, drawing his head out of the water, too. His face only a foot away flashed a smile clearly intended to disarmed her.

"Do...you...mind?" she asked. It wasn't a question. It was warning, but he chose to ignore it.

"I thought you might like to share the beauty of this place," he replied with an annoyingly sexy grin.

Treading water, she replied, "Perhaps under different circumstances."

He did a three-sixty in the water. "This isn't beauty worth sharing?"

"Eric..."

"Now that I'm here, it's the perfect opportunity to share this place. You know, get back the aloha."

"I'm not ready for that yet. I just want to snorkel and clear my head." Shoving the mouthpiece back in her mouth, clenching it with her teeth until she thought she might puncture the rubber, she dropped her face in the water and propelled forward.

To her dismay Eric stayed alongside her. A chill crept across her skin, so she swam toward the rocks on the edge of the break-wall of the monument and placed her palms on the warm flat surface, heaving her body out of the water in one swift athletic move. Not even the algae-covered sides of the rock slowed her down, despite her lack of a disciplined workout schedule. As she started removing her flippers, Eric heaved himself out of the water, in the same spot with the same economy of movement, making the muscular definition of his arms even more noticeable, if that were possible.

With cool water pooling at her feet, and the warm

tropical breeze fanning her wet body, she allowed her gaze to wander down to Eric's thick powerful thighs and well-defined calves. Again the palpitations of her heart increased.

So much for quiet contemplation. Impossible with a distraction such as this.

"Well, I'll leave you alone, then," Eric said, causing Nicole to halt her scrutiny of his magnificent physique.

"You're serious?"

He gave her a curt nod before removing his flippers and mask. As he started walking away, he surprised her when he reached out and touched her left forearm, long fingertips lingering for a moment, searing an imprint on her soul. "Be careful in the water."

"You think the sharks are going to get me?"

"That's not what I'm talking about. There are predators out there. Tiger sharks, yes. But we both know that's not what I mean. Keep an eye out, Nikki. Blue as lakes are the eyes of Blake's." His right palm brushed her flushed cheek. "Don't do anything to make those eyes glaze over, huh?" With that he turned away and disappeared through the dense Hala, Frangipani, Palapalai, and 'Ehaha ferns.

CHAPTER THREE

While standing in front of the white obelisk that formed the monument, contemplating the daunting task set before her, Nicole realized the afternoon sun had dipped low on the horizon. As she glanced around, lush Kāhili ginger, Hāpu'u fern, and guava bushes, and a spectrum of blue water lapping the lava rock-wrapped shore were the only things her gaze landed on. It appeared she was the only one who remained at the monument. All other sightseers were gone. Most, having also arrived by kayak, had left with the tide and plenty of time to paddle the lengthy distance back to the landing at the wharf before the sun dropped too low for good visibility. The large party-yachts, loaded with sunburned Midwestern tourists, had powered away hours ago, leaving her alone to reflect on the death of Captain Cook, her ancestor, although the lineage was through Cook's sister, and to figure out the truth about the final resting place of Cook's bones. Perhaps she could also give meaning to the death of her parents in the process.

She looked across the water at the high rock wall adjacent to the monument, wondering. Historically, Hawaiian burial sites were often in the steep, tall, vertical cliffs along Kealakekua Bay, and this one was rumored to be the hiding place of Cook's bones. The Hawaiians had laid him to rest somewhere up there for the intervening days between his death and when they had supposedly returned his remains to his men. But what if the bones the Hawaiian's had returned to Cook's men, which were placed in a coffin and dropped into the sea in a military burial, weren't Cook's bones? What if they were someone else's? They could have been any one of the other sailor's who had perished during that violent altercation in Kealakekua Bay so many years ago. Or what if the bones belonged to one of the Hawaiians that had been killed in the conflict? What if Cook's fleshless bones still remained in this cliff side?

Still suffering from guilt over her failed mission in Africa, she felt the stirrings of excitement at the prospect of another mission. A personal mission. She had to work through the pain if she ever wanted to be of service again, either to herself, or to anyone else. She had to revert back to her former self. Strong, confident, invincible. And Eric would not get in the way this time, no matter how difficult he tried to make things for her.

She had training. She had education. She had experience. But to be successful she had to shed her self-condemnation and self-doubt.

Grief had consumed her over her grandmother's

passing, and the bedside promise she'd made to Gran that day played a leading role in her disastrous failed mission. The intense mental distress caused her to make fatal errors, costing her entire team their lives, despite the fact that her case officer was convinced the accident was a catastrophic crescendo of mistakes that ultimately led to the downed plane. Escaping with a concussion, several broken bones, and the long gash in her thigh, she had been placed on involuntary leave-of-absence to recover. But physical recovery also meant she faced extensive questioning, even interrogation, by her Agency superiors, despite the position her case officer took. Over and over and over they asked the same questions in a hundred different ways, until they were satisfied that they had found their answers, escorting her to the edge of whatever lay beyond post-traumatic stress. As the mission leader, the Agency had placed the blame squarely on her. That was months ago. Cracking under the pressure, her engagement to Eric imploded, although neither of them had ever discussed what happened. He had simply disappeared when she needed him most. So she had been granted a long sabbatical. Then, once she passed a battery of psychological and physical tests, she thought she might return to the CIA. But only if it felt right. And if others didn't support her decision, they could make life even more difficult than it had been since that fatal crash all those months ago. Especially Eric. Unless his sudden reappearance in her life was a coincidence, which she strongly doubted.

But what was at stake if she *did* return to the CIA? There still remained one more month of leave, a month that might provide ample time to complete this personal quest to find Cook's bones, as well as give her time to decide whether to put both Eric and the CIA behind her for good. At this point, she had no idea what she wanted to do about Eric's sudden reappearance, but from a professional standpoint, the longer she was on leave, the more the private sector appealed to her. Starting her own intelligence and security agency had been a thought that had blossomed into strong possibility.

Two months ago, she intended to come to the monument as a spiritual journey to the resting place of her ancestor. It had drawn her there because of her grief and guilt. But now it was much more than that. It had become a way to fulfill the promise to Gran that she had been too despondent to expend any energy on until now.

Ever present was the sorrow of her losses weighing her down. The loss of her engagement. The loss of her work. The loss of the only mother-figure she had ever known. In fact, the only family she had ever known, having lost her parents at such a young age. Her team-members were the dearest friends she would ever have, and after months of grieving, perhaps it was time to move beyond the wretchedness. Otherwise this lack of focus would cause her to unwittingly encounter other near-death experiences until eventually one would finally claim her. Was that the final peace she longed for? Or did life still have meaning?

Her grandmother's voice in a recent dream had been like a salve on her aching soul, admonishing her for mourning to the point of paralysis. That voice alone gave her the fortitude to begin this personal mission. A mission that would bring closure.

The first drops of cool rain startled her out of her reverie as they splashed against her warm skin. Heavy drops. Weighted with an impending squall. Tendrils of hair had found release from her ponytail, caught in the breeze, tickling her face. The trade winds had altered, becoming more of a gale. Cool drops dampened the bright-orange sarong she'd wrapped around her chocolate brown bikini after snorkeling.

A chill ran down her arms as a sudden swell of water crashed against the rock wall along the water's edge. There was no safe way to kayak across the bay now. She'd have to wait it out.

Alarm crept over her. The golden sun had not only dipped low on the horizon, but it had also been obliterated by ominous black clouds hanging low and threatening, extending as far as she could see in every direction. The blue dry-bag in her kayak held minimal protection from the elements, although she still had one more albacore tuna lunch-pack left, plus a Snickers candy bar and a quart-sized bottle of Evian, which should tide her over for a few hours, but the real challenge lay in paddling back to the other side in the dark once the storm subsided. It was unwise, though, crossing the bay alone in the dark. And she didn't intend on taking any more stupid risks. None that could cost her life at least.

Dashing through the rain to her kayak took longer than expected. Concern flooded her brain as she scanned the spot where she'd beached it a couple hours earlier, finding only angry waves crashing on the rocks. Squinting against the pelting rain she noticed two yellow objects bobbing on the water about a quarter-mile off shore. In open water.

Surely that wasn't her kayak!

And what was the other yellow object? Another kayak? Yes! There were two kayaks tossing about in the turbulent waters, as if they had been tied together by a rope.

"Oh, no!" She dropped her face in her hands and expelled the air in her lungs. Then she pressed her fingers against her eyelids and said to herself, "Guess I'll be skipping dinner."

"I packed more than I need. Perhaps you might be interested in sharing with me," said the voice she'd recognize in a crowd of a thousand people.

Face still buried in her hands, Nicole turned and separated her middle and ring fingers to peer at the last person on earth she wanted to see in this latest predicament of hers. She dropped her arms at her sides, fists clenched. "I thought you left hours ago."

"I was hiking around the area and lost track of time." He pointed toward the horizon. "Looks like our transportation has been shoved out to sea."

Nicole rested her clenched fists on her hips. "Swept out to sea is more like it."

"Then the water would have had to come onto shore and up the hillside because that's where I dragged both kayaks before I started hiking."

"Mine, too? Well, that explains why they appear to be tied together. Geez, Eric, can't you just leave me alone?"

"We have bigger problems than me not leaving you alone."

Nicole rolled her eyes. "Meaning someone

deliberately stranded us? Don't be so dramatic."

"Could have been kids playing a game they didn't realize was so dangerous," he said as he rubbed his neck with the palm of his right hand.

As she gazed at the concern etched across his furrowed brow, she realized he wasn't just being dramatic. "But you think it was someone else?"

He gave her another intense stare, taking in her bedraggled appearance. "We need to make a fire and erect some sort of shelter."

She rolled her eyes again. "Oh, okay, Robinson Crusoe. And do you have matches in that backpack of yours, or were you just going to rub two sticks together? And while you're at it I'll have a rib-eye. Medium-rare," she muttered, shaking her head.

"Your sarcasm isn't going to dry you off, or warm you up." He dropped his backpack with a thud on a rock under dense branches of Hala and Frangipani trees, suggesting he had more tools in it than she thought likely. He unzipped it and dug around inside for a moment, then extracted something, which he grasped in his long-fingered fist. He glanced over at her, rotated his wrist then opened his hand like a magician. A red lighter lay in his open palm, and a gleam of satisfaction sprawled across his gorgeous face. "Eagle Scout. Remember? Prepared for anything."

"Right," she said, drawing out the word as she dipped her head slightly to one side.

"Grateful?"

"If I wasn't I'd be an idiot."

"Why can't you just say you're grateful?"

"I don't suppose you have a saw and a hammer and

nails in there, too."

"Never satisfied, are you. Just be grateful for what I do have," he said, shaking his head. "And start looking for a place to set up camp," he added with a jerk of his head toward the trees.

Survival training kicked in and Nicole decided it was prudent to set aside her prejudice long enough to search for something suitable for shelter, but when nothing appropriate presented itself, she decided they'd have to create it from the bounty of nature. And there was no time to waste. Branches and banana leaves were in great abundance. The problem was how to separate the branches from the trees. Upon further searching though, she found plenty of fallen limbs of Hala, Frangipani and 'Ohi'a Lehua trees, and gathered banana leaves for cover. Enough to create a shelter from the rain that continued to come down in weighted drops. Placement of the wet branches against the old lava rock wall of the ancient village site wasn't too difficult, but preventing the banana leaves from blowing away in the wind gusts proved a little more challenging. Recalling the stash of multicolored ponytail rubberbands in the fuchsia fanny-pack she'd clasped around her waist that morning, she realized they could serve as ties to secure leaves to branches.

She worked quickly and efficiently, but her back ached as she finished banding the last of the leaves and branches together. Placing her right hand in the middle of her back, she arched into a deep stretch, suddenly overwhelmed by a sense of sadness that their camp for the night had once been a thriving native village decimated by invasion and disease.

"I'll work the tightness out of your back after we

have a little something to eat," Eric said as he dropped an armload of kindling on the sand in front of the shelter.

A quick glance at his face made it apparent he was sincere in his offer. A helpful gesture to relieve her aching back. Nothing more. "Thanks," she said as he strode away. "Where are you going?"

He stopped and turned, eyebrows raised. "Do you care?"

"Well...I...yes, I do. It's getting dark." She pointed to his hand. "And you're the one with the lighter."

"And here I thought you just wanted that massage."

"You never answered my question."

"While you were playing Jane-of-the-Jungle, I was out gathering fruit for dessert." He allowed his gaze to wander over the shelter she'd built. "And an impressive job of it, too. It's obvious you've done this sort of thing before."

The muscles between her eyebrows drew together in what felt like an unbecoming frown. She shook off the suspicion that he was baiting her and stared him down, willing him to give in and retrieve his fruit.

She was just being paranoid. Even so, she could not afford to let down her guard. This was going to be a long, arduous night.

"Look, we're stuck together here. Don't think that flattery is going to change anything." She folded her arms across her body to project her most sincere 'back off' message, as well as to retain body heat, and inhaled the scent of the salt on the tradewinds.

He turned with a jerk and glanced at her over his shoulder, his eyes flashing with irritation. "I'm going to get fruit."

Eric must have stashed the fruit close to the makeshift shelter because he wasn't gone more than a couple minutes. When he returned, his arms were laden with red-hued guava, golden papaya, and two brown fibrous-husked coconuts. He set the ripe fruit on the rock under the banana leaves. Nicole forced herself to watch with indifference while the muscles in his tan arms rippled as his hands stripped the coconuts of their brown fibers. As if he was aware of her studious gaze, he glanced up at her for a moment, then unzipped a side pocket of his khaki swim-shorts and extracted the red lighter. He tossed it in the air and caught it with a swipe of his right hand, then looked at her with a gleam in his amber-green eyes. "Always carry the basics on your person." The beginning of a smile tilted the corners of his mouth. "But then you already know that, don't you?" His penetrating gaze held hers for a moment, creating an irregular heartbeat in her suddenly aching chest.

He shoved the lighter back in his pocket and began scooping sand aside with the heel of his water shoe, etching a place for a campfire before arranging the essential materials with concise precision. Coconut fibers on the bottom, leaves and twigs next, a few small branches on the next layer, then larger branches across the top. He glanced at her from where he knelt, waving his left thumb over his shoulder. "There's a lightweight plastic rain poncho in there. Go ahead and put it on. You look miserable. We'll dry off your sarong once the fire gets hot."

Why did his orders always propel her into response without question, she wondered, grabbing the poncho out of the backpack that was beginning to resemble Mary Poppins carpetbag.

Apparently satisfied that she was following his orders in silence for once, he pulled the red lighter out of his pocket again and with a quick flick of his thumb, a bright yellow and blue flame danced on the wick. He touched the flame to the layer of kindling. At first, the lighter did nothing more than encourage the wet kindling to smoke until he blew on it, causing embers to glow, then flames to flicker. As the kindling combusted, the fire began to glow in the darkening twilight.

Donning the orange vinyl poncho, Nicole sidled up to the warmth of the fire and extended her hands toward its increasing warmth, careful not to melt the poncho by moving in too close as the fire continued to grow while Eric added a few more Hala branches.

"Looks like you're making a bonfire," she said, still holding out her hands toward the flames, enjoying the smell of burning wood, and the feel of the heat that began penetrating her wet clothing.

"Don't want it to burn out before sunrise."

"With all this rain you'll have to sit up all night stoking it."

"I didn't intend on sleeping anyway."

She frowned as she glanced around. "I doubt there's any reason to keep watch. Even if someone deliberately pushed our kayaks out to sea, I'm sure they left along with the last of the sunlight. So unless there's something about yourself I don't already know, we should be fine."

The intensity of his gaze was suggestive. "You never know."

If she knew what he meant she might flee. But she didn't, so she stayed. She wondered, though, if he thought he already had his hands full ensuring her safety. Not that she needed his protection.

"What is that supposed to mean? Now what have you done? Something that would make someone purposely try to strand you?" She was starting to believe she really didn't know this man.

Her stomach growled. Something told her there were things she might not want to know.

"I think I just heard the dinner bell," he said as he rose from his crouched position by the warm fire. "How do you feel about beef stew and fruit?"

"Answer the question."

He pivoted on his bare feet until he faced her, gazing up at her while the flames danced behind him. "At the moment we're sharing resources, not information. Time enough for that after we have something to eat." With that, he leaned toward his backpack and started rifling through it again.

Not willing to let her question go unanswered, she waited until he'd pulled out a spoon-knife-fork set, chained together with an O-ring, and two foil pouches of freeze-dried beef stew. When her stomach growled again, loud enough that the geckos scattered, she decided she'd let him prepare the two-course gourmet meal and question him once his brain focused on digestion rather than her questions. His evasion of the issue meant he was concealing something and she intended to figure out what it was.

"Water bottle, please," he said, his long muscular arm outstretched, palm of his hand open in expectation. She placed the quart-sized bottle she'd set on the rock in his hand, watching the sinewy muscles as he grasped the plastic. As she watched him boil the water and add the contents of the freeze-dried packet, she took a deep breath. Any more deep breathing and she would start considering this a yoga workout. He would simply have to stop looking so...well...manly.

She glanced at the narrow shelter of tropical branches and leaves above her head. Unexpected panic swirled in her belly, almost crowding out the hunger. To keep dry during the night, they'd have to sleep sitting back-to-back, or bed down far too close together for prudence. Either way she might lose her sanity.

But her career had thrust her into far greater danger than sharing a narrow lean-to with a handsome rogue, even if he was her ex-fiancé. She could handle this minor crisis.

Unless he touched her.

At which point caution would be tossed into the blazing fire...to burn in ecstasy.

CHAPTER FOUR

"Dinner's ready." Eric dragged a short wet log under the shelter and sat on it as he stirred the contents of the foil pouch before holding it out to her. "You first."

She grabbed the cup, brushing her fingers against his. He ignored the zing of electricity that sparked between them again. Imagination working a triple shift. But he couldn't ignore how cute she looked huddled there in his poncho. He never realized how attractive survival gear could be. The appeal of vinyl was amazing under the right circumstances.

"Thanks," she said, averting her deep blue eyes. Maybe she felt the zing too. She wasn't one to behave like a Victorian virgin. So maybe it *wasn't* just his imagination.

"You're welcome," he said, noticing the enthusiasm with which she consumed the high-calorie meal once she was on the safe side of the fire. "Didn't you have lunch?"

She swallowed hard. "I only ate part of it. The rest of it I left in the kayak." She held up her palm toward him, the spoon intertwined in her fingers like a tiny baton. "Yes, I know better than to leave food behind." Her hand flew to her mouth and her brow furrowed.

"Something wrong?" He was confident she still had no clue why he was there, other than to make her life uncomfortable.

"Uh, no." She hesitated again, then added, "I left my digital camera and binoculars in the kayak too."

He could see that she was worried. Being stranded without hope of rescue by anything besides her own ingenuity had become second nature to her, despite the past. He couldn't figure out why, but for some odd reason she must have decided to wait until morning to hike out, as though her confidence had suffered over the course of the past few months. Well, he would wait, too. He had no idea what her next move would be, but he wasn't going to be too far behind when she made it. Keeping an eye on her had been an order. An order that had evolved into something personal, even though he'd been trained to keep his emotions at bay. Because she needed someone to protect her. And because he still had feelings.

Something about her lured him like a moth to a gardenia, despite their past.

An uncharacteristic vulnerability seemed to overwhelm her now. He'd flown her out of the wreckage of her failed CIA operation in Kampala, Uganda, and being the sole survivor must have taken its toll. With certainty, he knew she desperately wanted to block the accident from her memory, but that was futile.

The scene was so deeply etched in *his* memory, it could have just happened yesterday. As he stared at her across the fire, he saw flames licking the fuselage near the engines. In the frenzy to save them both before it exploded, he felt his heart connect with hers when her soulful blue eyes locked with his as she stared up at him from the relative safety of his arms. A moment later he felt her body go limp with unconsciousness, causing his brain to engage enough to propel his legs toward the helicopter waiting a short distance away. The connection he'd felt then made his arms suddenly ache to hold her again. Especially since so much time had lapsed. Despite the time-lapse, though, he still saw the same beauty in her that appealed to him when he'd first met her. But for now, he had to ignore physical desire and put his emotions on ice.

Timing was everything.

Blissfully unaware of Eric's train of thought, Nicole ate in silence, then passed the empty cup back to him. He was glad that she seemed to have lost the ability to read his mind.

"Thanks. That should satisfy my stomach for the night. But I wouldn't say no to a papaya after you eat some beef stew." Her sudden smile disarmed him. When he touched her knee she jerked away, making him grin like a Cheshire cat. On edge was exactly where he wanted her. If he kept this up she would refuse to share sleeping space with him, giving him the opportunity to stay on alert all night without her asking questions he wasn't prepared to answer. It would also prevent his heart from engaging in temptations it had no business even considering.

"Go ahead. Don't wait for me. I'll have some after I'm finished with this fine meal of freeze-dried camping packets. Yum," he said.

"It's better than going hungry."

"I won't argue with you there. Here's my knife." He handed her a Swiss Army knife equipped with everything but a glass cutter.

She whistled. "This is better than anything I've ever seen you use before." She paused, as though trying to think of some way to ease into a meaningless conversation. "I camp a lot now." Her half-smile melted the first layer of ice surrounding his determination to keep his distance. She was getting to him, regardless of how much he tried avoiding it. Language of the heart did not translate into self-discipline.

"And you never know when you'll need a corkscrew, right?"

Sweet laughter filled the air. This flirtation could lull him into seduction.

All of her attention seemed to focus on piercing the short blade through the skin of the papaya, but he wasn't fooled by her feigned concentration. They both knew she could filet that papaya blindfolded, with both hands tied behind her back and no knife at all. He was fully aware that the wheels of her mind churned while she strategized her next move. With training such as theirs, everything would be calculated. It had to be. Or it could be fatal.

"I saw you on the plane," Nicole said, lifting her gaze away from the fruit, locking it with his as pulp dribbled between her fingers. "A little ironic, don't you think, that we'd both be out here at the same time?"

So this was what she'd been mulling over? Wondering why he was there? "Coincidental, but what's so surprising about it?" he asked, hoping to throw her off his scent as long as possible.

"What's so surprising is that you and I were on the exact same plane to one of four popular Hawaiian islands in the enormous Pacific Ocean, where there are so many things to entertain yourself with you couldn't possibly do them all in a month. Yet we both end up at Cook's monument, on the same day, at the same time, and then both of our kayaks get shoved out to sea by "pranksters" before everyone vacates the area leaving us stranded together." Her hands paused in the air after emphasizing quotation marks with her fingers. She stared him down with those big blue eyes as she plunged her teeth into the papaya like it was her last meal. Finally, she swallowed, then said, "In my mind, that's not surprising at all."

"When you put it like that it does seem a little odd."

"Mmmmmm."

"What mmmmmm?"

"Why are you here?"

"I'm just another tourist enjoying a bit of nature."

"You're enjoying being caught in a squall, stranded on a peninsula where hiking out would be doable, but incredibly miserable in the dark?" She rolled her eyes. "You're enjoying this?"

"Okay, enjoying might be a stretch, but I'm waiting until morning to leave. I have no intention of hiking out now. I've been on that trail before and as you said, it isn't all that much fun. And attempting it in the dark is asking for trouble."

"But you said you didn't intend on sleeping."

"And I don't intend on hiking out in the dark either." Eric busied himself with cleaning off the utensils they'd shared, hoping she'd drop the subject. He wasn't ready to make up a story about what he was doing there. Lying to her would only created bigger problems. History had proven that to him once before. And the truth was definitely something he couldn't disclose.

For the second time in his career, he felt personally involved. He'd saved her life. It felt personal, even though he knew it shouldn't. Even though they'd almost gotten married.

Eric watched Nicole shoot another glance at the narrow spot of fine cool beach sand beneath the tropical shelter she'd erected. It was obvious her nerves were stretched to the snapping point. If he intended on staying up all night, perhaps she could curl up there and get some sleep. Even though it couldn't be very late, she looked as though exhaustion had clutched her very soul. And he figured she hadn't really accomplished anything she'd set out to do, except visit the monument. Losing her digital camera and high-powered binoculars, along with the rented kayak, also meant she couldn't get any closer to the cliff wall either, since it was encompassed by water. It appeared there were large holes in the cliff, but were they big enough to contain a grave? Eric couldn't really tell from where they had beached their kayaks hours ago. And if the holes were large enough, did one of them house Cook's bones, as the CIA suspected? The same bones he knew Nicole had promised her

Gran she'd find and return to England?

Eric overheard the Hawaiian man on the cement wharf brag about *his* grandmother knowing where the bones were, and he knew that information made Nicole more determined than ever to solve the mystery before someone else found Cook's bones. When she got back to the wharf, she would ask that man about his grandmother. It was the only lead she had at the moment and it might be worth exploring. But for now, she had to get through the night with him, a man he knew she still found disturbing, even if she refused to admit it.

The bright-orange cotton sarong she'd placed across the lava rock must have finally dried out because she rolled it into a ball and shoved it behind her head and leaned against the rock. Not the most comfortable position, but she looked so tired she must have been beyond caring. The vinyl poncho was large enough to envelope her like a sack to retain body heat, which probably was waning by now, so he was happy to see she had decided to keep it on. Eric wanted her to feel a sense of trust and confidence in him. Maybe in her exhaustion her memories could be suspended long enough to forget the pain he'd caused her. Having been trained to listen to intuition, he was sure Nicole was certain that he was still a man of strength and courage and that she could sleep knowing he was around. But just why he was around was another mystery he didn't want her solving at the moment. Faint memories flitted across his thoughts at the sight of her, but rowing across the bay, snorkeling, hiking and gathering and prepping food had begun to catch up with him, so he thrust his mind into neutral.

He felt her gaze on his head and glanced at her, causing her to drop her line of vision to her knees curled up against her chest underneath the vinyl poncho. "Go ahead. You look beat. Get some sleep," he said.

She rolled over on her side, her back to the lava rock and tucked the sarong under her left ear. If she felt anything like he did at the moment, closing her eyelids would feel wonderful. Sleep was a luxury he could ill afford, though. The sight of her kept him from considering what might happen if he submitted to the call of the Sandman, too.

CHAPTER FIVE

A strand of hair, teased by the fragrant breeze, brushed Nicole's nose, waking her from restless slumber. The clouds had cleared. Rugged coastline surrounded the bay, looming large under a full moon. The delicate fragrance of pikake flowers wafted through the leaves overhead. Lava rock glistened in the moonlight as gentle waves lapped across the hardened black surfaces. Tiny sparks danced upward when a heavy green branch fell across the crackling fire.

And Eric was nowhere in sight.

Nicole bolted upright. Alarm coursed through her veins. Then she remembered where she was, and that she was safe simply by virtue of her sheltered location within the village ruins. Kealakekua Bay was protected by lava where guava bushes, lush Kāhili ginger and Hāpu'u ferns and Frangipani and 'Ohi'a Lehua trees flourished. She was in relative isolation, unless someone rowed across the bay in the dark, or climbed down the steep hillside above. Since the full moon shone bright as a setting sun, it was possible for someone to arrive during the night, but she doubted anyone could do so completely undetected. Yet she'd slept through Eric's departure, so perhaps she'd gone into a deeper sleep than she should have while exposed to the elements. And who knew what else!

After a slow luxurious stretch that started with her toes and extended through her neck, she decided to hike out rather than wait around like a damsel in distress. Despite the relative safety, she felt exposed. She wouldn't get another wink of sleep if she remained inactive. Besides, it was ridiculous to stay here. The bright moonlight would make her escape much easier.

While wrapping the bright-orange cotton sarong around her waist underneath the poncho, she dug her toes into the fine cool beach sand. With a couple of swift kicks with her right foot, she flung as much sand as possible across the fire-pit. As the last embers flickered and died, she turned to grab her flip-flops and fanny pack.

"What the *hell* did you do that for?"

"Eric! I thought you deserted me!"

"Why on earth would you make that leap of logic? And why did you just bury the fire under all that sand? Now I'll have to rebuild it." He dropped his backpack and shook his head muttering, "Women!"

"Don't bother rebuilding it on my account. I'm hiking out."

"Not alone, you aren't. Rule number one, never hike alone."

"Since you're the only other person around, you'd

better grab your backpack then and follow me."

"Rule number two, never hike in the dark when you don't have to. Do you even know where the trailhead is? And what's your destination?"

"Napoopoo Beach, where my car is parked. I know there's a trail leading up to the main road from here, but if we cut across that," she pointed to the top of the steep cliff, "we'll end up at the beach on the other side of the place where we dropped the kayaks in the bay." Since doubt began etching a map across his handsome face, she added, "The trail to the top is doable. Rugged, but doable." It seemed necessary to convince him to join her. As he pointed out, it wasn't wise to hike alone.

"Right. Doable if we stay on that rugged, almost non-existent trail. If we venture off, who knows?" He pointed to her cheap rubber flip-flops. "You intend to hike that trail in those things? That's just plain stupid. I'm rebuilding the fire. We're waiting until morning."

"Do not call me stupid."

"Then you're welcome to join me in a sanity check," he said, folding his arms across his chest. "When the sun comes up we'll bribe someone to give us their two-man kayak and we'll row across the bay."

She mimicked his posture by folding her arms across her chest, too, and screwed up her nose. "I've hiked through much more difficult terrain than this coastline, and I don't intend to let a poor choice of footwear keep me from doing so again. Besides, it isn't that far."

"I don't think it's the distance that should bother you. Improper gear can lead to all kinds of problems. You'll have blisters, or twist your ankle, at the very least." He stopped short of stating the obvious problems with what he clearly thought was an idiotic idea.

She looked down at her feet, pivoted her left ankle, modeling the flimsy bright-pink rubber flip-flops for his benefit. "I live in these so I doubt they'll give me blisters. And I know where the trailhead starts. This way," she said as she began pushing her way through the trees into denser growth of Koster's Curse, not caring now whether he followed or not. She was wide awake. Daylight was still hours away. And a lot of ground could be covered in the intervening hours.

Nicole smirked when she heard Eric's sigh of disgust, which she assumed could be translated as surrender. Without turning around, she knew he was hot on her heels. After ten minutes of silence, picking their way through the thick vegetation surrounding them, Nicole plucked a white ginger blossom that had brushed its white silky petals against her forearm. Its heady perfume permeated the air as she tucked it behind her right ear. She turned to Eric. "See? Piece of cake. And spectacular! Even at night."

"You say that now."

"Yes, I say that because I'm fine. What about you, poor thing, being dragged along against your will?" She pointed to his footwear. "Your sandals aren't any better than my flip-flops."

He chuckled. "Unlike yours, mine have thick rugged soles and nylon straps guaranteed to secure them to my feet. They're trail-runners, built for this type of terrain. You could step right out of yours at any given moment."

"Like I said, I'm fine."

"And stubborn."

"I'm going to ignore that. You could have stayed behind and saved me the pleasure of your complaining."

"Complaining and stating facts are two entirely different things."

As the trail continued to climb, their breathing became labored, yet it didn't slow Nicole down. "How's the pace for you? Can you keep up?" she asked.

In reply, he reached underneath her poncho and placed his hands on her bottom. The lightweight sarong and skimpy bikini fabric were so thin, she could feel his palms tense when her muscles contracted at his touch. "As you can tell, I'm having no difficulty whatsoever," he said, although Nicole thought he sounded short of breath.

In response, she increased her pace. He didn't laugh, even though she knew he wanted to. But he did cough. The sound was muffled by the dense overgrowth, then carried away on the tradewinds, but he kept it up until he started actually coughing.

"Serves you right. And try to keep your hands to yourself," she said, slowing the pace a tiny bit. Enough to give him time to catch his breath.

She was still a woman of surprises and secrets. She wouldn't let him discover them all. And this was only a passing flirtation, if she let him continue to flirt, since they both still traveled unencumbered by relationships. Relationships only led to bondage. She'd escaped him once before and she wasn't about to succumb again. Not if she could control herself.

Her waning attention snapped back to their

situation when she veered off the trail. Tall grasses grew between enormous chunks of broken lava rock creating an obvious shortcut destined to lead them across the top of the cliff, cutting miles from a hike that would only become more treacherous, judging by the vertical terrain looming in front of them.

"Nice to have a little moonlight for this pain-in-the-ass stroll," he said as he glanced up at her again.

"Suck it up, princess," she said.

His laughter brought a reluctant smile to her dry mouth.

A few minutes of labored breathing passed as they continued their hike. "So what's your story, Flyboy?" she asked.

"My story?"

"Yes, your story. You know, the usual. My parents were killed under suspicious circumstances when I was young, which led me to join the CIA, etcetera, etcetera, etcetera. That story. Riveting conversation is the only thing that will shorten this hike. Talk to me. Why were you on a plane with me in Africa? What else have you been doing since you left me stranded?"

"Is that *your* entire story? It's old. Give me something new that I don't know," Eric said.

"I don't have anything new."

"We both know that can't be true, but tell me more about your parents."

"You're evading my question about Africa. And I'm sure you know about as much as I do about my parents. They were killed when I was young. My grandmother raised me, but she never discussed what happened to them until the day she took her last breath. She mentioned there were suspicious circumstances."

"Sounds suspicious."

"Please don't joke, Eric. According to my grandmother, they left me with her so they could go on a second honeymoon and were vacationing here --" She paused for a moment and turned toward him, but her gaze was on the ground. "Close to Kealakekua Bay, as a matter of fact, on a sixty-five foot yacht. After nightfall, another boat approached and opened fire. Of course they were killed, but the crew survived and were brought in for questioning. Gran said they thought the crew was in on it and it was some sort of a setup."

"What happened?"

"Robbery was the official declaration." She turned toward the path again and resumed hiking in her inappropriate footwear. "The sad part is they had nothing onboard worth being killed for."

"You said you were young."

"Four."

Eric frowned as he kept pace with her. "Too young to remember them very well. That's terrible, Nikki."

"It *was* terrible. And I don't really remember them anymore. All I have are photographs my grandmother gave me." She paused. "And her stories."

"What did they do for a living?"

"My parents? My dad was a professor at the University."

"The University?"

"Here, in Hawai'i."

"What did he teach?"

"Anthropology. I Googled him once." She laughed. A mirthless, sad sound, even to her own ears.

"Curiosity."

"And what did Google reveal?"

"Nothing my grandmother hadn't told me already."

"What was your dad working on?"

"When they died, he was on a sabbatical. He and my mother were vacationing. I have no idea what he was working on, but Gran told me before she died that my parents' deaths had something to do with Captain Cook's bones. She said they hadn't all been returned to his men after he'd been killed back in 1779. She believed to her dying day that my parents had the bones on the yacht with them when they were attacked. She made me promise to find the bones, Eric." She hesitated for a moment, then continued on the trail. "Avenge their deaths, she told me." Nicole stopped again and turned toward the bay, her deep blue eyes searching the horizon as if looking for the ghost of that sixty-five foot yacht. "Can you imagine what kind of pressure Gran has put me under?"

"Is that what you're doing here?" he asked.

Did he really not know? Did he want her to keep talking so he could learn all of her secrets? Expose herself to him? History had taught her it was prudent to only give him so much.

Shrugging, she turned to the trail again and began walking. "It's crazy, I know. But I promised Gran I'd at least try. I have no idea if the story is true. Gran had a strong heart, but dementia set in. She may have even dreamed the story about my parents. Captain Cook was our ancestor and for religious reasons Gran believed his remains should have been buried in the same grave as his wife, as was the custom in those days. So I promised her I would make that happen."

She heaved a sigh. "A deathbed promise is such a burden, especially when you don't know how you can keep it."

"So you're here to find the bones and get them back to England?" It was more of a statement than a question.

"Cambridge, yes."

"You're right. That's a huge burden." He hesitated, then added, "She's gone now so you're absolved, I'm sure."

Nicole halted in her tracks.

"Or not," he added.

It was pretty obvious that Eric realized he'd said the wrong thing as soon as it came out of his mouth. She knew him well enough to know he'd endure the chastising he deserved, especially since he'd have done the same thing if *he'd* have made a deathbed promise. Except he was alone in the world. And made promises to no one. She should have known that when he'd asked her to marry him.

"You heard the part where my parents were killed because of the bones, right?" The heat in her tones could have ignited the tall grasses surrounding them.

"Allegedly killed because of the bones."

She turned, fire in her glare. "Doesn't matter if it's alleged, or not. They were killed. And I intend to find out what they had on that yacht that was worth the price of two lives."

"You've let an awful long time pass between then and now."

"I heard the story for the first time while Gran lay on her deathbed. That was a year ago." She paused. "And I haven't been able to start looking until now."

CHAPTER SIX

Eric knew Nicole's parents had the bones on their yacht when they were killed. That was why he was here. To prevent her from getting killed too. The value of the missing bones seemed to elude her. She was too focused on taking them to England. There were others who wanted them too. For less than honorable reasons. Which put her life in jeopardy. His too, now that he was protecting her. And she seemed oblivious to that fact.

They came to a Y in the trail. To the left, the trail continued up into the tall trees, and eventually to Napapoo Road. To the right, the trail aimed for the top of the steep cliff overlooking Kealakekua Bay. By following the cliff top, they would save hours of hiking and come out close to where they had left their vehicles. It made sense to follow that path, if one could call it that.

The sound of the surf crashing on the rocks below reminded him why he didn't like this idea. Footing had become difficult. He noticed Nicole had been able to keep the bright pink flip-flops on her feet, despite the fact that it had become difficult to traverse the hillside without slipping on sharp black lava shards.

"I was enjoying the quiet until the tropical storm blew in. I should have noticed the subtle change in climate. I've been distracted lately. It's become a habit I can scarce afford to indulge in," she admitted.

Apparently, she had no idea how *little* she could afford to be distracted, Eric thought. "There's a fair chance of twisting an ankle here, so clear your mind and stay focused on this for the time being," he said.

"With nothing but moonlight to light this almost non-existent trail, we'd be better off using night-vision goggles." She stopped again and turned toward him, her face shadowed by tall grass filtering the bright moonlight. She giggled. The sound was loaded with stress rather than mirth. Remaining silent, he realized she probably still struggled with post-traumatic syndrome.

"No night-vision equipment in my backpack, I'm afraid."

She turned and continued picking her way across the uneven ground. "It was no coincidence that you showed up at Cook's monument at the same time I did, is it? Why, Eric? I'd appreciate it if you'd level with me."

"You're right, Nikki. It wasn't a coincidence. It's because of our past. I couldn't get you out of my mind." Eric grinned.

While still pressing forward, Nicole waved. "Something my grandmother was fond of saying was 'hooey!' I'm calling hooey on that."

"Watch your language! And keep going. We're still quite a distance from our vehicles."

Nicole stopped and turned, moonlight reflecting in the glint in her eyes. She frowned but didn't utter a word before turning back to the trail. She continued up the trail.

Eric noticed now that about every third step Nicole stumbled, then she'd catch herself. It was obvious she was exhausted. So was he, come to think of it, especially since he hadn't slept at all. And she'd probably only gotten about two hours of sleep, if that.

They continued picking their way across the gnarly cliff where prickly Kiawe trees consumed the curvature of the hillside before dropping off the edge into the bay. The trail they were following must have been carved by hoofed creatures. They were so close to the edge that one misstep and one, or both of them would plunge over the side into the deep dark waters below.

Nicole stumbled again.

"Watch your step," he said, reaching forward to grab her left wrist as it swung in rhythm with her stride.

"Thanks, but I'm fine," she said, twisting her wrist out of his loose grasp without breaking her stride.

"Tired?"

"A little. You?"

"A lot."

"Try to keep up anyway," she said, causing him to laugh out loud.

She stumbled again.

Picking up the pace would have been something Eric would have expected of her on the trail, but she didn't. Instead of issuing another unspoken challenge she started maintaining a slower pace. Much slower than when they'd begun this insanity a little more than two hours earlier.

Half-way across the cliff, at the highest point of the apex, an enormous horned silhouette suddenly appeared in the tall grasses.

Startled, Nicole jumped backwards.

Into thin air.

CHAPTER SEVEN

The pores of Nicole's exposed skin tingled as the wind skittered past her. Training kicked in. Rotating her freefalling body, bile rose in her throat.

Bam! Against the cliff. *Bam! Again!* Breath whooshed through her pursed lips. Blood oozed on her tongue.

The taste of fear.

Awareness heightened. Her battered body plummeted down the rocky slope in slow motion. She squinted. The ginger blossom that she'd tucked behind her ear now spiraled toward the sea, its heady scent evaporating as it floated downward.

Flailing her hands and arms, she clutched at Kiawe branches jutting from the rock, choosing pain over death. Her body slammed. The Kiawe's sturdy trunk became an extension of her hand. But could it hold her weight?

The scream inside her head deafened her. She'd pierced her skin. The only sound that escaped her lips was a sharp intake of breath.

The animal trail above lay in silence. Had Eric fallen to his death?

Dark memories flooded her mind. Jagged metal spearing her thigh. The intensity of the heat from burning jet fuel.

Compared to that, this wasn't so bad. Even though it felt like she'd wrapped her fist around needles.

She sucked in another breath and assessed her situation. Endorphins shot through her bloodstream, relieving some of the pain.

Inch-long needle-like thorns covered the Kiawe tree that had broken her fall, thorns that lodged themselves nearly through the palm of her right hand. Four of them.

She hung on. The weight of her entire body dangled beneath her.

Ignoring the pain, she swung her body toward the tree. Additional puncture wounds were unavoidable. This time she permitted herself to grimace as the needle-like thorns stabbed her calf. She didn't care. It was better than the alternative of freefalling two hundred feet to her death.

"Reach your left hand up as far as you can and grab hold," Eric said from somewhere above her, suggesting he hadn't followed her over the edge.

A quick glance up shifted her body enough for the thorns to tear through her skin. Her instinct was to scream at the pain. Instead, she remained silent, conserving energy so she could stretch her free hand above her head in an effort to grasp the rescue object he had lowered to her. The skin on her calf ripped again. When she felt the metal carabiner, she yanked it hard enough to wretch the attached rope from Eric's grip. But he held fast.

"Wrap it around your waist, then clip it. When you're ready, I'll pull you up."

"Oh, no problem," she muttered under her breath, amazed at the equipment he had in his backpack. Thank goodness he insisted on following her up the trail. Otherwise she'd still be dangling on the needle-ridden Kiawe tree as daylight broke.

"You can do it, Nikki. Just clip the rope around your waist."

"This tree has very, very long thorns on it."

"I know. A Kiawe tree isn't the best thing to break a fall."

"You are a master of the obvious. It hurts to move."

"The longer you hang on the worse it'll be when you let go."

"Right," she said. She stuck the cold metal clip in her mouth, then clamped her teeth on it.

With her left hand she pulled the rope down on the right side of her body, forming a small loop. Her right arm burned. Each tug on the rope felt as though her shoulder would rip from its socket. She took a deep breath, the clip still clenched between her teeth, and reached around her waist with her left hand. The rope dangled a little too far from her fingertips, yet with her right elbow she somehow caught the loop. In one swift move, she swung the rope toward her waist and grabbed it with her left hand.

"Tug on it when you have it clipped around your waist."

Her calf and right hand had ceased throbbing.

Small relief that endorphins were finally doing their job. But the thorns had to be removed soon, or she'd have bigger problems.

She pulled the loop around her. The clip, still clenched in her teeth, opened easily as she slid the rope inside. A quick glance at the breakers two hundred feet below confirmed that ascending the cliff face was the only way out.

"Almost ready?" Eric asked. Anxiety and concern weighed his tone like a stack of gold bullion.

"Once I get unstuck I'll tug on the rope. It may take a moment though. And there might be screaming involved."

"At least you still have your sense of humor."

"The jury's out on that," she muttered.

Tears began to flow unchecked as she braced her dangling foot against the cliff side, attempting to get traction. "Pull me up about a foot," she called.

The gentle tug on the rope fired excruciating pain throughout her body. The rope slipped over her breasts before coming to rest at her armpits. But it positioned her high enough so she could extract her right hand from the thorns still attached to the tree, without putting all her weight on her calf. The poncho had become an obstruction, but there was no way now to shimmy out of it. Besides, she'd need it once she got to the top of the cliff. Her core body temperature had dropped, given the trauma she'd just put it through.

She extricated herself by wrenching her hand out of the thorns in one swift movement, stifling the impulse to scream at the top of her lungs. An unintentional yelp escaped her lips, though, when she yanked her calf from the needle-like thorns.

She took another deep breath, then shouted, "Okay. Pull."

Eric began to gently tug her up the cliff. She lost her flip-flops in the fall. Bare feet were all that prevented her body from bashing against the rocky surface. Involuntary shudders shot through her. Agonizing pain accompanied every slight movement. Finally, after what seemed like many long hours, Eric reached down, grabbed her under her arms and heaved her up over the edge.

On firm ground, she lay on her side for a moment. A tear escaped and rolled down the side of her cheek, into her hair, as he unclipped the rope and dragged it out from underneath her.

Twenty-five feet from the edge of the cliff where she'd gone over, Nicole saw what had nearly caused her demise. A huge cow with an enormous head stood watching her with interest, still chewing its cud. If it didn't hurt so much she might have laughed out loud at the absurdity of it all.

With a gentleness she'd come to expect from Eric, he picked up her right hand and examined it. Blood oozed from four deep puncture wounds. Then he examined her calf with careful fingers. Without saying a word he searched his backpack again. No doubt for first aid supplies. Thank goodness the man was prepared for anything.

Another stifled moan slipped past her lips as he dressed each puncture with antibiotic ointment, then wrapped both her hand and calf in white gauze before securing it with first aid tape.

"That should get you back to civilization," he said,

sitting back on his heels, his amber-green eyes awash with unidentifiable emotion. "But I see you've lost your fabulous footwear."

"This is the hike from hell," she said, wiping her hands across her cheeks.

"I hate to tell you, but we've still got a little way to go. And this animal trail --" he glanced over at the cow, then continued, "--is littered with broken lava rock. You can't keep going in this condition."

"So you think I'm spending the rest of the night with her?" she asked, jabbing her thumb in the air toward the cow. "Absolutely not." With that declaration, she grimaced as she rose and hobbled in the general direction of the beach, still two hundred feet below, ignoring the pain in her raw bare feet. After all, the pain in her feet paled in comparison to the pain in her hand and calf, not to mention the rest of her body.

She kept reminding herself she'd been in much, much worse situations than this. At least this time no one was chasing her. Or shooting at her.

Relief overwhelmed her as the ground began to slope downward, indicating they were almost back to the beach. Until the drop changed from a gentle slope to a steep bank.

She stumbled.

Eric snatched her left forearm, forcing her to stop. "You can't continue like this. Look at your feet!"

She glanced down. "I'm fine."

"Oh, for the love of my country!" he exclaimed as he shrugged off his backpack. "Get on my back."

"So we can both go tumbling down this slope? Yeah...no."

He snatched the backpack off the ground and slung it over his shoulders, then stuck his thumbs under the straps and shifted it until it was centered on his back. "You can't continue walking. Your feet have to hurt. Just cooperate for once."

She shook her head and started walking again. When he scooped her up with his arms it shocked her speechless. But her feet did feel like ground round.

Now the pain in her calf throbbed with every step he took. Her aching hand lay limp against his muscular chest. Through the thin fabric of his tee-shirt his heartbeat felt strong. Steady. Like home.

Disappointed in her line of thought, and the fact that she had to be rescued yet again, she didn't dare squirm or resist. Otherwise they might both end up toppling head-first down the hillside. And she'd had enough of *that* for one night.

Sometime in the early morning, arriving back at the parking lot at Napoopoo Beach was the greatest pleasure she could remember since she'd left there yesterday morning. Riddled with holes, blood oozing from her wounds, she looked at Eric with trepidation and asked, "How am I going to inform the kayak rental company about their kayak?"

"If that's all you're worried about you're definitely in shock." Instead of putting her down, he carried her to his vehicle and set her bottom on the cold hood, her legs dangling down the passenger's side. She winced. "You're one tough woman," he said, fumbling in a zippered pocket on the backpack for keys before he unlocked and opened the passenger door.

In the gentle warm tropical breeze, Nicole noticed leaves rustling. But a gentle breeze wouldn't cause the palm fronds and banana leaves in front of Eric's aging Land Cruiser to shudder with such vigor. The branches rustled as if mongoose were dancing on them.

Heightened awareness seemed to suspend physical discomfort. As Eric leaned toward her to lift her off the hood she leaned into his chest, ignoring the smell of sweat and salt and whispered, "Someone's watching us."

"I know. Grab my neck and wrap your legs around my waist," he whispered back. His arms tightened like a vice, making her wince. "And kiss me with hot passionate desire." He slid his hands between the cool metal of the SUV and her bottom. All pain forgotten, a gasp hissed past her lips. She turned her face toward his. "Make it good," he added, his hot breath fanning her lips as she anticipated the sweet torture.

Time stood still.

Eric raised his head after the passionate kiss. Had he not been positioned between her legs, pinning her to her perch, Nicole would have slid off the vehicle as she melted under his seductive touch.

A chill seeped through the poncho as the slack between their bodies broke the temporal illusion her mind had conjured up.

Time shot by in a flash.

Without hesitation, he whispered into her ear, "Whoever it is will think we're lovers." Then once again, without warning, he possessed her lips with such bold craving she'd almost been convinced of the exhibition herself. If she pressed any closer to him she would no longer be aware of where she left off and where he began. And for a moment, the temptation disconnected her resolve.

Until the palm trees rustled again.

Eric must have heard it, too, because he cupped her bottom and slid her off the hood of the Land Cruiser, hugging her close to him while her ankles locked around his waist and his lips continued to assault hers. She slid her hands down, draping her arms across his broad back, feeling the sharp breath he sucked in. His deft move around the open passenger door, while their tongues did the habanera, made Nicole wonder just how practiced he was at such maneuvers. In all her years of experience she'd never resorted to this to escape danger.

Depositing her on the tan leather seat with care, he whispered, "You're pretty damn good at this." Then with one swift move he closed her door, dashed around the vehicle to the driver's side, wrenched open the door and jumped in, rotating the key in the ignition before he'd even pulled his left leg inside. He slammed the door shut, shoved the gearshift into reverse and backed out, then shifted into 1st. Sand sprayed as he stomped on the gas, creating a cloud of dust. As Eric sped away from the beach up toward the paved road without so much as a glance her direction, Nicole held her throbbing hand in the air and reached across her body to clutch the passenger roll-handle with her left hand.

"Where are we going?" she asked.

"It's 3:30 in the morning. We're both exhausted and I don't know about you, but sleep is about the only thing on my mind now."

"Really?" No red-blooded male could be focused on sleep after a heated make-out session like they'd just experienced.

"Where are you staying? I'll take you to your hotel."

If he wanted to pretend he wasn't aroused, then she would do the same. "What about my rental car back there?"

"Later."

If she hadn't been on the verge of collapse, if her body didn't ache with a vengeance and if they hadn't had an audience for the past fifteen minutes, she'd have driven herself back to the cottage. Obviously, the kiss was only a way to deflect attention. It meant nothing to him. But once again, she hadn't been able to resist his chivalry. In fact, she was grateful for it.

Which was so unlike her.

"You never said where you're staying."

"The cottage on Tiger Hiroshi's Plantation," she replied.

"Okay."

"You know it?"

"I spend a lot of time on the Big Island. Of course I know it."

When they pulled into the long driveway, weariness overwhelmed her. With the cottage in sight, all she could focus on was how great it would feel to crawl between cool sheets and shut out the world. A world which now included Eric again. Suddenly, she didn't have the energy to wonder what he thought or did. Or if he was only pretending he felt the same passion that had threatened to consume her a little while ago.

"Just drop me off here," she said, as he slowed in front of the cottage.

"No way," he said, glancing across at her, his

amber-green gaze filled with concern. "You'll sit right where you are until I park this thing and come around to carry you inside." He stopped the vehicle, shoved the gearshift into park, shut off the ignition and jumped out. Through the open window he said, "You're feet must hurt like hell. Got a first aid kit in there?"

"I have no idea," she said, opening her door with her left hand, still holding the right one in the air. The throbbing had begun again. All she wanted was a respite from the longest night of her life. She didn't care if there was a first aid kit in the cottage. She only cared about dropping her weary head on a down-filled pillow.

"Don't even think about getting out of this rig without help," he said before hustling around to the passenger side to make good on his word.

He carried her into the cottage and set her on the bed as if she were a Ming vase, then went in search of a first aid kit, which he discovered under the sink in the bathroom.

As he cleaned and bandaged her wounds again, she fought back the tears that threatened to overflow. Pain had become more acute. She appreciated his weak attempt at distracting her by extolling the virtues of the cottage.

"You have a charming place here. That bathroom is as big as the bedroom. It's very pretty, too. Perfect place for a vacation. Except it's too secluded."

"Seclusion is exactly why I booked this place," she said, glancing around the charming cottage, with its white lace curtains, antique furniture and resident lime-green gecko climbing the wall at the foot of the bed. She couldn't even remember the last time she'd been able to enjoy a paradise such as this. She wasn't about to tell him she'd dipped into her meager inheritance from her grandmother in order to indulge in this small luxury. Her work took her to exotic locations, but she never saw the beauty. Only the danger. For once she wanted to see the beauty. But now it was all in vain.

Nicole added, "There are ten acres to this property, an incredible panoramic ocean view, a swimming pool, and such abundant fruit trees, you can pick your own breakfast. Being half mile off the main road makes it perfect for someone looking for peace and quiet. If you saw it in the daylight, you'd know what I'm talking about. It's beautiful. Serene and beautiful," she said, wondering why she felt compelled to convince him of anything until she'd had at least five solid hours of sleep.

"And it's exactly why you're not staying here alone."

"Because you want to see it in the daylight? Come back later. I'm too tired to entertain," Nicole said as she flopped back on the pillow yawning.

"Because it's too isolated. I don't think it's safe."

"I don't need a bodyguard," she said, her eyelids drooping. She rolled her blue eyes. "This isn't the first time I've stayed here alone. I can assure you, it's perfectly safe. The caretakers are friends of mine. And if it makes you feel any better, their house is about half-way between here and the main road." She tucked a lock of shoulder-length blond hair behind her left ear. "Besides, I can defend myself." She jutted her bruised chin in the air. "If I have to."

"I'm sure you can, but it doesn't matter. It isn't safe for you to stay alone in such an isolated place. Trust me on this, Nikki."

"Because --?"

"Just trust me. You're not staying here alone."

She held up her bandaged hand in surrender. "Fine. Take the futon in the living room." She pointed to the cedar chest at the foot of the antique iron bed. "There are extra pillows and blankets in there. Help yourself. I'm going to sleep now. Nite-nite."

The last thing she thought about before drifting into a delirious dream was how she was going to tell the kayak rental company she lost their kayak and couldn't afford to replace it.

CHAPTER EIGHT

Eric watched her close her eyes like a sleepy child. With a tentative hand he brushed a wayward strand of blonde hair from her brow. Her mouth dropped open as she slipped into deeper sleep almost before she'd stopped bossing him around. Freedom to study her face without reproach seemed too good of an opportunity to waste.

Long eyelashes, tips bleached from the searing rays of the sun. A perfectly shaped nose that tilted at the tip. Luscious lips split open far enough to reveal white pearl enamel. Thick flaxen hair spilled across the pillow like a warm ray of sunshine.

If he ever felt inclined to get involved with someone again, she would be the candidate.

But that wasn't why he was here. He was here to protect her, even though she didn't know it. And wouldn't appreciate it if she did.

Life began mocking him from the moment he'd been tasked with helping her find Cook's bones. It mocked his resolve to never get personally involved again. It mocked his ability to remain disconnected. And worst of all, it mocked his determination not to love anything.

Eric sat for another moment, watching Nicole sleep while he considered the possibility that they'd been tailed to the cottage, or at least as far as the drive off the main road. When they left the beach, he'd noticed another set of headlights turning onto the road. Suspicion grew when the vehicle paced them to the turnoff from the main road. Regardless of his speed, the other vehicle remained far enough away that he couldn't make out the make or model.

Contemplating the possibilities, he decided their tail had to be Doyle, the retired CIA agent, or Collins, the ex-MI6 British agent, or both, if they'd figured out a way to work together without killing each other. Doyle had been engaged in research, so he had said, at the British Museum on another case the same year Nicole's parents had been killed. Soon afterward, Doyle retired from the CIA under a cloud of suspicion that he had made a practice of using diplomatic pouches in various parts of the world to smuggle enough drugs to supplement his government retirement. And it was also rumored that Doyle had recruited Collins. It wouldn't surprise Eric if the two of them were looking for Cook's bones, too. If they found them first, the Hawaiian Hereditary Front would be first in line to take them off their hands. For a price. HHF members wanted to return the Hawaiian Islands back to Hawaiian blood members, reestablishing a new monarchy, a monarchy that would be controlled by the corrupt top members of the HHF. The bones would give the HHF's leadership great ritualistic power to rally the many Hawaiians steeped in dreams of past gods and glory. No doubt, it would inspire their members, as well as others who were still undecided about the HHF. And if the HHF wouldn't meet Doyle's and Collins' price, Eric knew without a doubt that the two ex-agents would put Cook's bones on the free market. The word on the street was that an unidentified, unscrupulous, wealthy Chinese man had been putting out feelers for the bones for years, for their historical value, as well as the magical powers they were purported to possess.

Eric was sure the two rogue ex-agents possessed enough knowledge and weaponry to annihilate any obstruction to their acquisition of Cook's bones. And they would use them on anyone who got in their way.

The FBI, as well as the CIA, had suspicions that Doyle had instigated the attack on Nicole's parents. But there had never been enough proof to bring him in. And Collins had gone underground about the same time. Had they gotten away with murder? Both men were probably pushing sixty now. But Eric didn't doubt for a moment they were anything but capable...and deadly.

All those years ago, after the violent death of Nicole's parents, the bones had vanished once again. Their informant within the HHF said there was never any mention of the bones being recovered. The wealthy Chinese man still had his offer out on the street. Which most likely meant neither Doyle or Collins had been successful in their endeavors back then.

So who had the bones?

Eric knew Doyle and Collins were still out there. Still out there searching. Not only for the bones, but for anyone who might possess a single wit of knowledge about them. And Eric knew they were closing in. He felt it in his gut.

Avoiding these two rogue ex-agents might be more challenging than running across molten lava.

While all this raced through his brain, Eric rose from the edge of the bed, tiptoed into the living room and pulled out the futon. Then he tiptoed back into the bedroom and removed the necessary bedding from the cedar chest at the foot of the bed where Nicole lay in innocent slumber. If he could save her from the danger that lurked beyond these cottage walls, he would. He knew she'd been in firefights, and he knew she was brave. He couldn't stop her from risking her life, but at least he could try to prevent these predators from massacring her.

Like they had her parents.

When this was over Nicole would value his partnership more than ever.

He just wasn't sure if they'd both still be alive when it was over.

*　　　*　　　*

"Good morning," Nicole said, as she passed through the living area into the kitchen, clenching her teeth with every movement. "I smell coffee."

"Hazelnut blend. Help yourself."

Raised eyebrows was her only reply.

"Okay, I helped myself." His grin reflected no apology for making himself at home.

Every muscle in her body must have been aching from the beating she'd taken on the hike, but she was trying not to let it show. Instead, she turned her back to him, probably thinking he hadn't seen the pained expression on her face as she poured a cup for herself.

"I'm surprised you're still here." She glanced at him over her right shoulder and added, "Especially since you look like you're ready to head out for the day."

"I've been up for a while." It was none of her business that he'd dozed a grand total of fifteen seconds during the short night. Forty-eight hours without sleep was no great record. He'd gone longer. Not that he could maintain a sharp mind and quick reflexes with much more sleep deprivation, but he was okay for now.

"Did you sleep at all?"

"Some."

"Meaning none?" She limped across the kitchen and sat down on the far end of the forest-green futon that he'd already folded into its upright position. Her feet disappeared beneath the sarong she still wore as she wrapped her left hand around the navy-blue mug and took a sip.

"Meaning I'm fine."

His heart rate increased as she licked a drop of moisture from her upper lip. Sleep deprivation had made him weak after all. Six hours of shut-eye skipped to the top of his priority list.

"As soon as you finish with that maybe we should see about the kayaks. What rental company did you use?" he asked, averting his eyes from her sensuous tongue as it played with her lower lip, making him want to kiss every square inch of her, starting with that exquisite mouth.

"Wild Coast Kayaks. You?"

"Ironic name considering what happened," he said, his left-brain reengaging. "Mine came from the same outfitter. That'll make the whole thing easy."

"You're kidding, right? Easy explaining what happened? What part of that will be easy?"

"I didn't mean it'll be easy to explain what happened. I meant it'll be one stop." He tried disarming her with his smile. But it didn't quite work. He could see she refused to be taken in by his manly charms, although he was hoping to prove he was useful to have around. No matter how handsome he was, how sexy, how rugged, she resisted his appeal.

"Do I have time to shower?" she asked.

Eric wanted to think she intended to put some distance between them before his magnetism thrust her headfirst into insanity. He glanced at his Shinola Argonite watch and nodded.

*   *   *

After showering and replacing the soiled bandages covering her throbbing puncture wounds, Nicole made a brief attempt at looking feminine as she studied her reflection in the seashell-bordered mirror. Considering the fact that she barely owned lip-gloss and mascara, the attempt to look feminine would be rather...hasty. Without a doubt, the man sitting on the forest-green futon in the next room appreciated beauty. He probably had his fair share of gorgeous women dangling about his neck like expensive jewelry since their engagement ended, but that was of no concern to her now. Since she'd never taken much time for makeup in the past, as she left the bathroom she wondered why she was suddenly lamenting over the lack of lipstick in that moment.

Dressed in clean white linen shorts, a turquoise gauze blouse and a pair of sturdy white sandals, she stood by the front door and asked, "Ready to chat up the kayak shop owner?"

Eric glanced up from a women's lingerie catalog. "You look rested." He studied her for a moment, then added, "And quite lovely."

"Thanks." She shifted her slender frame from one foot to the other, inexplicably embarrassed at his comment. "My legs, feet and hands hurt, but I'm fine."

As he shoved himself off the futon, he tossed the catalog on the end table and said, "There are a few things in there you'd look rather sexy in."

"Uh-huh. Go ahead and order them for me," she said. "I'd be happy to model them for you." She rolled her eyes and shook her head before turning away.

"I just might take you up on that."

"Very funny. Let's go, Flyboy."

Explaining the situation to the kayak rental company hadn't been as difficult as Nicole had expected. Apparently they weren't the only ones with a similar experience yesterday. The owner of Wild Coast Kayaks said there was a reason he'd chosen that name for his company. According to him, his kayaks usually washed ashore somewhere on the island a day or so after a storm, like the one that hit the island yesterday afternoon. With waterproof identification on each kayak, ninety percent of the time the strays were returned to his shop. So much for Eric's suspicion that they'd been someone's target for mischief.

That resolved, Eric took Nicole back to Napoopoo Beach to take care of item number two on their list.

Collect her car. When his Land Cruiser rolled to a stop at the rear of her rental car, she hopped out and slammed the door. She placed her left hand on the open windowsill and said, "Thanks for the ride. And thanks for patching me up. And you know I was kidding about the lingerie, right?" She tapped her palm on the sill. "Okay, then." Waving her left hand in dismissal, she added, "See you around."

"Hey, hold on, babe. I'm not that easy to get rid of. After all, if memory serves me, I did rescue you. You can thank me by going out to dinner with me tonight."

A grimace flickered across her face. "Can't. I've got some things to do before I head back to Honolulu."

"Such as?"

"Such as none of your business. Just because you think you rescued me doesn't mean you're entitled to a reward."

"I never said I was entitled. I'd just like to have dinner with you."

"We did that last night, remember?"

"You can hardly call that dinner. That was eating out of a foil pouch. *Dinner* is served at places like the Kona Inn. So how about it?"

A brief hesitation was all he required to make assumptions he shouldn't, but Nicole acquiesced when he said, "Great, I'll pick you up at the cottage at six-thirty. Dinner at seven." After all, it would be entertaining, if nothing else, but she couldn't let him think she was an easy target either.

"If I'm not back at the cottage at six-thirty, go ahead without me," she said.

Rich laughter coated the interior of his Land Cruiser. A frown drew her blond eyebrows together.

"I'm serious, Eric. I might not be back by six-thirty," she reiterated.

"You'll be there."

She leaned her forearms on the window sill and squinted at him. "You are without question the smuggest man I've ever met. What makes you so certain I'll do as you say?"

"Because you'll be hungry by then and the prospect of a charming dinner companion, who is willing to lavish attention and nourishment on you, will be too great a temptation to resist." The smile he flashed her rivaled any toothpaste commercial ever filmed.

"Do you practice this stuff in front of a mirror?"

Eric shoved his stick-shift in reverse and began rolling backward. "See you at six-thirty, babe."

Nicole jumped away from the vehicle, then slammed her clenched fist on the hood as he continued to grin at her with smug satisfaction.

"In your dreams, Flyboy," she said softly as he continued to back up. No way was any man getting away with ordering her around in a relationship. Not that this was any sort of a relationship, but she wasn't even continuing a pseudo friendship with a man who would deliver orders and call her 'babe' like she was some play thing, or object of lust. She was a professional, a CIA operative who had taken advantage of a leave-of-absence to satisfy a promise to her grandmother. She was *not* a vacationing bimbo looking for a handsome hunk to coax her into a holiday fling that would leave her heartbroken as she returned to a boring desk job in some remote embassy. Her life was already more exciting than parachuting from the moon. This romantic tête-à-tête style of excitement held little interest for her. She had too many other things to accomplish. Like chatting up the bragging Hawaiian man who helped her drop her kayak in the water yesterday morning. Now *that* was not a waste of time. It was imperative research to the discovery of Cook's bones.

Even she wasn't above covert tactics when it was merited. But Eric's continued resistance to divulging his recent past, and explaining the remarks about flying with her in Africa left her uneasy, as well as frustrated.

Once Eric had driven out of the parking lot and headed up the hill, Nicole limped over to where the Hawaiian man had been sitting on his lawn chair in the back of his tan beater pickup truck the day before. Since he wasn't there now, she figured he might be assisting someone at the water's edge, so she limped across the park-like setting and glanced at the wharf. But he wasn't there either.

"Can I help you?" asked another Hawaiian man in a faded sleeveless tee-shirt, grimy cargo shorts, and dark reflective sunglasses perched on his thick brown nose. His long thick hair had been pulled into an unkempt ponytail, strands of wiry hair escaping over his ears. "Pull your car around here and I'll help you get your kayak in the water," he said making a circular motion with his beefy arm, apparently oblivious of the fact that she possessed no kayak. Nicole noticed the small "HHF" tattooed on the inside of his right bicep.

"Uh, no. I'm not kayaking today. But do you know where that other guy is, the one who helps people drop their kayaks in the water?"

"Which other guy? There are several of us out

here." He waved his arm, indicating two others, also available to provide assistance. Which meant yesterday she'd been too immersed in her own thoughts to notice *this* peculiar Hawaiian, who by no means blended in with the others. This one was different. His persona exuded power and control. Not something typically associated with the men who hung around all day long working for tips.

Failure to take in her surroundings yesterday, and the people that occupied them, was in direct conflict with her training. Had she lost her edge?

"There was another guy here yesterday," she said.

"We are the only ones here, miss. Any one of us can help you." His voice had dropped in pitch, almost unnoticeable, but Nicole picked up on it. He knew where the other man was.

"The one I'm talking about is the guy who sat on that pick-up bed," she said, pointing to the empty lawn chair on the bed of the truck. "Yesterday morning he was sitting there."

"Oh, Huko? Well, as you can see, he's not here. He's probably restocking his booze, or something. What do you need *him* for?"

"Oh, nothing. Thanks for your help. Some other time, then." Instinct told her something was wrong with the missing Hawaiian man with the toothless grin and weathered skin so dark and rough it could be mistaken for saddle leather. Now wasn't the time to try to figure it out, though. Not with this man issuing subtle unspoken threats.

"What do you want with him?"

Nicole frowned. It seemed as though he had blocked her path. The subtle menacing hostility was palpable, although he didn't say or do anything specific to openly suggest he was threatening her.

She limped backwards a few steps. "Nothing. Nothing at all except to thank him for helping me yesterday." Turning for a brief moment she waved farewell.

The man's dark aura had her on high alert.

It was ominous.

She would come back later in the afternoon. Perhaps he would have packed up and pulled out by then and the man she wanted to question would have returned. Although judging by her instincts, and the hostility from this man, she wasn't sure what she'd find when she returned. At the moment, she wasn't even sure she *should* return.

Still exhausted from her nighttime escapade, she decided to relax for a few hours during the heat of the afternoon, sitting pool-side at the cottage with a six-month-old fashion magazine she'd found. The images held little interest for her, but it was a way to pass time as she dozed in the warm sunshine, for once enjoying the simple pleasures of life. Mynah birds chirped in the banana trees bordering the pool on two sides. Idyllic relaxation was just what the situation warranted, especially since she'd have to hit the ground running as soon as the sun dropped lower on the horizon. She'd wait to go back down to the bay until the bragging Hawaiian man had finished helping everyone pull their kayaks out, but not so long that he'd be gone for the night. But she also wanted to time it so the hostile guy with the 'HHF' tattoo had gone home for the day. She had no desire to encounter *him* again. He felt dangerous. And her intuition was never wrong.

Warm sunshine caressed her skin. The fashion magazine slipped to the ground. She dozed.

Drenched in sweat, despite the cloud cover that shielded her from the sun, when she awoke she knew exactly what she had to do.

CHAPTER NINE

Green-cushioned teak lounge chairs situated beside the royal-blue tiled swimming pool took advantage of an unobstructed panoramic view of the ocean. During her afternoon nap on one of the chairs, her dreams were so vivid that when she woke she expected to see Eric hovering over her battered body lying beside the wreckage on the lush green hills of Africa.

He was a CIA operative. A pilot. Sent to rescue stranded or downed spies.

And he had rescued her.

Which meant he was here now for purely professional reasons. Plain and simple.

She had been knocked unconscious in the crash, and suffered several broken bones. And that gash. That hideous gash on the inside of her thigh. She fingered the deep furrow of the scar.

Her dream. Her nightmare.

The same nightmare she'd been having for months. Yet Eric hadn't starred in it until this afternoon.

Why now?

She considered the options, none of which made her happy. What if he'd been sent to keep an eye on her? What if they thought she was about to cross over the edge of sanity? What if they thought she would expose the failed mission?

What if he'd been sent to silence her?

No, she thought, tossing that one out. He'd had ample opportunity. He would have already done that by now. Which meant there had to be another reason he'd become her self-appointed watchdog.

Was he keeping tabs on her for personal reasons? Did he think she needed protection. His protection? He seemed to focus a lot of attention on her safety.

Or what if he were stalking her?

She shook her head. Why on earth would he stalk her? That idea didn't make any sense, either.

Would she ever uncover the truth behind his motivation? After all he was a CIA op, too. Honesty wasn't an overriding characteristic. But now that she considered it, did she even want to know the truth?

What if he followed her because he was after the bones? Cooks bones?

Perhaps she *would* be at the cottage at six-thirty, dressed and ready for that dinner date. It would provide the perfect opportunity to disguise her questioning under the cloak of flirtation. But she'd have to be ingenious to outfox him.

A quick glance at her watch told her she'd have to wait to visit the bay again, and the Hawaiian man, if she was going to be prepared to meet Eric on time.

When he knocked on the cottage door at six-fifteen her hand was poised to apply a light coat of mascara to the tips of her blonde eyelashes. She decided to keep him waiting on the doorstep until after she'd also slid a wand of newly-purchased pale-pink gloss across her lips, smacking them together in leisure, causing him to knock a second time. Patience never seemed to be one of his overriding characteristics.

Pretending she was delighted to see him was her greatest weapon at the moment, so she hiked up her hot-pink sarong skirt another inch and re-knotted it on her right hip. Then she tilted her chin down, and with her left hand, tousled her hair and draped a lock across her left shoulder. Donning a seductive smile, accompanied by a come-hither glance, she opened the door.

And if his dropped jaw was anything to judge by, she'd just positioned him in checkmate.

"You look..." He cleared his throat and began again. "You look ravishing," he said, after regaining his composure. Ten seconds that made her aware of the power of her feminine wiles. No wonder women could destroy empires without so much as stepping out onto the street beyond their doorway.

"You're early, but that's okay. I'm hungry."

His expression suggested he'd been hypnotized by the radiance of her seductive smile. He was hungry too, but she suspected food was not what he was thinking about at that moment.

"I figured you would be," he said after obviously shifting his thoughts from below the belt to above the neck.

Pushing the door open she limped across the threshold onto the sidewalk between the cottage and driveway. When he scooped her up in his strong arms with fluidity, her lips pursed.

"Easy, Flyboy. I can get to the car without being manhandled," she said, splaying a hand across the light-blue linen fabric stretched across the ripcords of his chest.

"This is not manhandling," he said, a twinkle in his amber-green eyes. "I'm displaying my gentlemanly charms."

As his arms encircled her with the intention of drawing their bodies into an intimate embrace, she realized she wasn't the one in possession of the power. Had he not been carrying her at that moment she would have collapsed at his feet. The realization humbled her. But the feeling was not so overpowering that she decided to surrender to it. She possessed her own skills. Skills that she intended to employ. She'd just have to wait for the right time.

The drive to the Kona Inn lasted a little longer than she anticipated and making small talk while she strategized seemed a great waste of valuable energy. Idle chatter never held much appeal, but since he'd re-entered her life she seemed to engage with increasing frequency. Under normal circumstances, every sentence, even every word would be calculated to deliver its message with concise intent.

However, this was anything but normal circumstances.

The Kona Inn was modest, but was situated at the edge of the sea, which made it an exceptional location. An outdoor patio provided a stunning view of the setting sun. For their amusement, spinner dolphins frolicked just offshore, leaping and twisting mid-air before splashing on the surface of the azure water.

As they sat down to dinner, Nicole decided it was time for a serious discussion. She would enjoy watching him squirm like a gecko had crawled up his shorts. She waited until the waitress had taken their order and brought their drinks and dinner.

"When are we going to talk about the wreckage in Africa?" Nicole asked in a low tone as the waitress moved out of eavesdropping range.

Eric shifted in the cushioned rattan chair as if the imaginary gecko had indeed crawled up his shorts. She flashed him a brilliant smile, enjoying his discomfort, then leaned forward and took a sip from the lavender straw perched in the ice that hosted a small purple orchid floating in her Mai-Tai. She glanced up at him and fluttered her eyelashes. And waited.

When he picked up his fork and jabbed the ring of pineapple he'd pulled off his teriyaki chicken, she decided he wasn't going to respond. But then he glanced around the open-air restaurant and leaned toward her as if to share a confidence. In a hushed tone he said, "We'll discuss this later, babe."

She leaned toward him, eyes flashing and rasped, "A person who cared would be comfortable discussing it now, *babe*."

"And if I do? What then?"

She glanced down, picked up her fork and began raking the tines through the rice on her plate, creating a Zen garden. The icy glare in her eyes was intended to warn him he'd have to draw on years of training to extract himself from this current snare.

"You know why I'm here. And I don't need your help," she said, still dragging her fork through the rice.

"Mmmmm...that's an odd statement, considering."

"You know what I mean."

"Considering you'd probably be dead right now without my help, babe."

She waved the fork at him, flinging a few grains of rice across the table. "Stop calling me 'babe'. I am *not* your babe. Not anymore. The name is Nicole. Use it."

He held up both hands in surrender. "Whatever you say, Nikki."

She rolled her eyes and shook her head, then finished her meal in silence. Without a doubt, he had the upper hand. And she knew it. But she wouldn't give in. No matter what. It was obvious her persistence frustrated him, but she could tell there was no way he was going to divulge anything.

Nicole changed her tactics and began a running monologue on the beauty of the islands, the temperate climate and the condition of the economy as he finished eating, all topics requiring no response from him.

She assumed he had some sort of an assignment, but it appeared the lines were blurring between what was professional and what was personal. He seemed obsessed with protecting and seducing her. Which was unacceptable. She couldn't let him get to her again.

Every time she glanced across the table at him, the fire in his flashing gaze suggested the passion he'd tried letting go of. It was obvious she made him feel uncomfortable, especially now that she seemed resistant to his magnetism.

During the quiet drive back to the cottage, deep in thought about how she could use this to her advantage, she almost didn't notice the vehicle in the side mirror.

"You just passed the driveway to the cottage," Nicole said, craning her neck to watch the driveway disappear around a curve in the road. When he accelerated she glanced across at him. "Now what?"

"We're being followed."

"You mean that car back there?"

"They must be after you then because I'm no threat to anyone now that I've been forced to take a leave-of-absence."

"But you're looking for Cook's bones," Eric said, glancing across at her with furrowed brows.

She frowned. "And that's of interest to whom? He's been dead for over two centuries." She folded her arms across her chest, ignoring the pain in her hands. "If someone is chasing us, they're wasting their time, and they're not very aggressive."

"They don't think so, in case you haven't noticed." He negotiated another sharp curve in the road, then added, "This is the second time in less than twenty-four hours."

"*What?*" She turned in her seat to face him, her expression mirroring her feelings when he spared a quick glance her way. "And you didn't think it was important to mention it the first time?"

"It didn't seem necessary."

"On the way to the Kona Inn?"

"From the bay this morning." Strong, long-fingered hands gripped the steering wheel as he swung the vehicle around the next curve, then jerked it hard to the right onto a dirt trail obscured by the lush overgrowth of banana trees. He shut off the headlamps and taillights. Enormous leaves slapped against the Land Cruiser as they bounced further down the narrow trail in absolute darkness until they rolled to a stop on a slight slope amidst rows of coffee bushes. Eric cut the engine. He rolled down the hand-crank window on the driver's side with his left hand as he held up his right hand to silence her. Not that it was necessary. Field experience induced reflexes essential for survival.

Eight minutes of silence passed.

"You were following me this morning?"

Eric fired the engine, shoved the gearshift into reverse and began maneuvering the SUV backward. "They're probably long gone by now."

With all the jostling on uneven ground, Nicole's hand flew to the dashboard. "No one followed me to the cottage this morning. I'd have noticed. And with the tight curves in the road, in order to see us back out now, they'd have to be within twenty-five feet of where we went into the trees. I'm sure they're long gone."

"For now."

"I'd like to know who is so interested in Cook's bones." She set her right elbow on the passenger windowsill as Eric turned the headlamps and taillights on and backed the SUV out onto the pavement, now facing the opposite direction from where they had just come. "And why," she added.

Eric's glance surveyed her with astonishment. "You really don't know?"

"No. But as long as we're driving around, would you mind going back down to the bay? The Hawaiian man I mentioned last night wasn't there this morning when I went back to talk to him. Maybe he's camping down there tonight. I'd like to ask him more about what his grandmother told him."

Eric slowed, then pulled into the next dirt driveway and made a three-point turn. "You realize the more questions you ask, the more unwelcome attention you're going to get."

"Who cares?"

"You do recall being followed...twice...right?"

"And you think that's because I'm asking too many questions?"

"You've heard of the Hawaiian Hereditary Front?"

"Of course. They're trying to reinstitute a monarchy," she responded. The fragrance of gardenias wafted from the hillside, infiltrating the vehicle through the open windows. "Isn't that lovely."

"Yes, lovely." He glanced at her again. "Absolutely lovely."

"The scent of gardenias, Eric."

"So you know some of the leaders of this crusade are not altruistic. Rather like oh-so-many before them, all they want is power. Control over others. Because many of the Hawaiian natives have secretly continued to worship their old gods and practice the old rituals, their leaders know that possessing Cook's bones would be a great symbol of power. Magical power. With the capability of invoking the old gods' power to smite their enemies, meaning the United States, the British, the Chinese, etcetera, etcetera, etcetera. They believe they will reclaim the islands for the Natives. But in order to exhibit these magical powers to do this, they must first find the bones."

As they pulled into the parking area at Napoopoo, Nicole looked around for the Hawaiian man. He was nowhere to be seen, nor was his tan beater pick-up truck parked in its usual spot. No surprise. It was dark, and all the kayakers would have returned long ago. The man seemed to have vanished, perhaps back to some hovel nearby.

Eric pressed his warm palm on her knee and continued on. "The Kona coast is probably full of this secret underground society of full-blood and partial-blood Hawaiians, seeking to overthrow the state of Hawai'i so they can declare it a sovereign nation again. They believe the Hawaiian's were sold-out in the late 1800s."

Nicole frowned, recalling school lessons and stories Gran had told her. "That was when the Mahele divided land between the King, the ali'i and the people, permitting private ownership of land for the first time in Hawaiian history," she said.

"Some saw it as a great reform, but this secret society of the HHF sees it as the single event that led to the downfall of the kingdom during Queen Lili'uokalani's reign. Natives were homeless overnight while large amounts of land went to influential businessmen and misled regents. Very few of the common people got any land from the Mahele, or subsequent Kuleana Land Grant Acts," Eric added.

"I remember Gran saying the shares the monarchy and government received were either sold, or transferred to European and American planters. I can see why they feel wronged."

"There are varying opinions on the intent of land reforms in Hawaii. Today, the HHF is angered by who benefited years ago, and who should be held accountable now."

It was beginning to dawn on her the danger and

challenge of her situation. "So the less-than-altruistic want to find the bones that would give them magical powers."

"Knowledge of the ancient chief's burial place has most likely been handed down from father to son of the head Kahuna's blood-lines, and the present-day Kahuna is determined to overthrow the state and re-instate Hawaiian rule."

"But how can Cook's bones bring any power whatsoever over the people?"

"The head Kahuna intends on inciting the Hawaiian brotherhood by using them in secret ceremonies that will make the Hawaiian warriors invincible. That, and a lot of Paco Loco, if you ask me. Rumor is, he intends to overtake the Hawai'i armories on each island, starting with the Big Island."

"And you're here on a covert mission."

"I care about you, so I'm here to protect you."

"Like my Gran said, that's a pile of rotten hooey, Eric. You don't care in the least about me. You were sent. You're here to make sure I keep my mouth shut about what happened in Africa." The sudden realization made her aware that she had repressed both her sanity and her intuition. She should have recognized Eric's intent as soon as she'd seen his face again.

His hand hesitated on the door handle. "Nikki --"

She buried her face in her hands and shook her head. "I don't believe this," she said, before grabbing the door handle and yanking it open.

Stumbling out of the vehicle, Eric was at her side before her foot hit the ground, placing a muscular arm around her shoulders. "We're in this together. We'll find Cook's bones."

She shrugged out of his tender embrace and began striding toward the cement wharf. "Oh, I bet '*we*' will. But for whom? The government? As soon as we find them, you'll take off with them. And I'll be left empty-handed. I'll have nothing to fulfill the promise I made to Gran." She shook her head averting her gaze from his. "Thanks for the offer, but no thanks. I'm on my own." Bitterness and anger flashed in her eyes. "Let the games begin."

As she turned away, he grabbed her forearm with strong fingers. "If we don't team up, one of us is going to end up like this poor sucker," Eric said, spinning her around.

Despite her anger, her glance descended on a dark mass floating just at the water's edge.

CHAPTER TEN

Nicole sucked in a hissing breath as Eric reached for his cell phone and dialed 911.

"It's him," she said, shuddering. "I know it's him."

Eric held up a hand to silence her, then relayed as many pertinent details as possible to the 911 dispatcher. Then he grasped Nicole's shaking hand in his, pulling her toward the Land Cruiser, helping her as she collapsed on the passenger seat. "Him? Him who?" He stood in the open doorway, his large hands resting on the top of the doorframe watching her with intensity.

Arms across her chest, she rubbed her hands up and down her biceps, chilled despite the warmth of the fragrant tropical breeze, and the pain in her wounded hands. "It's the Hawaiian man with the pickup. The one who helped me get my kayak in the water yesterday morning."

"The one who said he knew where the bones are."

She nodded. When she glanced up at him her eyes

were filled with anguish. "I had no idea anyone would die over this."

"You mean anyone else."

"Besides me?"

"Your parents. And probably a few others over the decades. These bones hold more power than you realize."

"So what's next?" Her glance had become more of a glassy-eyed stare, which began to worry him. "I just want to get the bones back to England."

"But you're not fully prepared to fulfill this deathbed promise, Nikki."

"Why not? My parents thought it was important. Why should their death be any more in vain than my own?"

"Because it was a long time ago."

"Not so long ago that my grandmother forgot."

"She's gone now, too. You're the one out here like a boar upwind of a shotgun."

"You don't have to do this with me. I've been in situations much worse than this before and survived them. I can do it again."

"I have no doubt all your missions were smashing successes." He grimaced. "With that one last exception."

"It was smashing alright. A series of fatal errors set in motion before I was even aware of them. And it wasn't just my mission that failed."

"Which is why you need my help now. You realize this poor guy floating in the bay knew more than he was supposed to, right? My guess is an HHF's, or someone else's interrogation session ended with him spilling his guts, probably out of unmitigated fear.

Someone has been watching him, listening to every word he said, following anyone who interacted with him so they could report back to the head Kahuna." He shook his head. "Apparently the big man decided to have him silenced."

"So they're probably the same people following us."

"A safe assumption."

"What if they come back while we're waiting for the police?" she asked, feeling a little uneasy now that she had come to her senses.

"What if they never left the bay?"

"You mean they could be watching us right now?" Panic had to remain suppressed.

"It wouldn't surprise me."

"But they won't attack because they'd rather follow us."

Eric nodded. "To the bones."

"So you think they failed in extracting the location out of this poor guy, huh? Then they still have no idea where they are, either," Nicole stated.

"I'm sure if it was someone else, they would know only of their value. And whoever it is, I wouldn't count on them using the discovery of the bones for anything honorable. If the bid on the black market is higher than what they can get by selling them to the HHF, they won't care that they're forfeiting their beliefs by doing so."

"But if they do that, they'll be murdered just like that poor guy back there," she said, jerking her left thumb toward the dark water behind them.

"I'm sure it's a risk they're willing to take. That's why we're teaming up. I'm not leaving you alone."

"Very macho of you, Flyboy, but in case you've forgotten, *we* don't have any idea where the bones are, either."

"I'm sure they're wondering why you spent the night out there on the point." It was his turn to wag his thumb in the air toward the general direction of Cook's monument.

"And why I keep coming back."

"Yeah. Looks like you know something. So they'll continue to stalk you until they get what they want."

She sighed. "Fine." She stuck out her bandaged right hand. He accepted it with a gentle caress in consideration of her throbbing puncture wounds. "I suppose I should thank you for this."

"My pleasure. Really," he muttered under his breath with a sexy grin as he turned toward an approaching police car. She wasn't sure she liked the idea of spending every waking moment with this handsome specimen.

They watched in silence as the police plucked the body from the water and laid the Hawaiian man on the cement surface of the wharf. The coroner approached as a photographer snapped photos. Standing near the body, Nicole debriefed the police on what she knew, confirming that this was the same man who had assisted her with her kayak deployment the previous morning. The expression on the dead man's contorted face suggested terror had been his last thought before death.

Which meant someone wanted him silenced.

Permanently.

Once they had exchanged information with the police, Eric drove Nicole drove back to the cottage, keeping a watchful eye for any tailing vehicles. Velvety moonlight remained their sole companion during the fifteen-minute drive.

Nicole unlocked the cottage door, glanced at her watch. "I know it's late, but I'm sure I won't be able to sleep. I picked up a bottle of wine on my way from the airport the other night. Care to join me for a glass?"

"Great idea." Since they hadn't been followed, she felt comfortable indulging in this simple pleasure with him in close enough proximity that he could provide additional security. With his handgun stowed under the futon in his backpack, she figured he could get to it without difficulty, if necessary. And she didn't want to be alone.

Eric watched her uncork the bottle, obviously enjoying her sommelier prowess.

"I can feel your penetrating stare." A broad sexy smile curled her full lips as she turned toward him. His sheepish expression shouted '*busted*'.

He moved in, pretending to assist her with pouring. But it was obvious that what he really wanted to do was shut out the images of a brutal world and ravage her with passionate kisses. Let come what may. Life was short, as evidenced by bodies floating face-down in dark seas.

As he approached her side, though, she turned and placed a slender hand in the center of his chest, giving him a light shove backward. "Easy, Flyboy."

His hands rose in mock surrender. "What? I was just coming over to help."

"Oh, yeah, because I need help lifting this bottle."

"Well..."

"If we're becoming partners in the hunt for the bones, I need you to be straightforward with me. What are you really doing here?" she asked, her eyes searching his face for the truth as she leaned her backside against the counter and handed him a wine glass half filled with an Argentinean Malbec.

A subtle groan escaped his lips when their fingertips met. Was it the innocent touch, or the interrogation that elicited the response? Whatever the cause, she enjoyed watching him squirm again.

"You're kidding, right?" he asked.

Raising her left eyebrow a fraction had the desired affect.

He sighed. "This doesn't leave the cottage."

She held up her left hand. "Hey, what happens in this cottage stays in this cottage."

"In that case," he said, reaching for her.

She twisted away from him before he made contact. "It was just a figure of speech."

"Can't blame a guy for trying."

"Back to your story."

He shrugged. "Fine."

"Fine." She sipped her wine.

He sipped his.

"Go ahead," she said. "I'm waiting."

He took another sip of wine, then said, "For obvious reasons, the FBI doesn't want the HHF to end up with Cook's bones. They know what happened to your parents. I'm sure you're aware they know your grandmother died a year ago, too. Not to mention they know you're now on a self-imposed mission to find your ancestor's remains." He waved his arm toward the wall of windows overlooking the water.

"And you just witnessed what happens to people in the wrong place with the right information."

"Okay. I get all that. It still doesn't explain why you're here." She glanced around, then added, "In my cottage."

"Drinking your wine."

"Drinking my wine, yes. Why are you here, Eric?"

"The truth?"

"Try it. You'll like it."

"But *you* might not."

"Eric!"

He held up both hands in surrender. "The Agency sent me to protect you."

"And what happens when we find the bones? Are you going to let me take them to England? Or is your real mission to take the bones to the mainland?"

"The FBI has been tracking the HHF for years. But Cook's bones didn't become an issue until one of our CIA agents discovered an ex-MI6 agent has been conducting extensive research on them, discovering their spiritual and historical importance." Eric fingered his moustache. "Remember that rogue agent from way back?"

"Oh, Colin something. No..." Nicole snapped her fingers three times. "Collins." She wagged a finger at Eric. "William Collins."

"William Collins, yes. The CIA has been tracking his movements too, because of his past."

"Which includes a joint mission that went sideways in a god-forsaken area, if memory serves me. And didn't Collins walk away untouched with a mysterious increase in his wealth, while our CIA agent lost a couple of good contacts?" Nicole asked, her eyes widening at the memory.

"Which infuriated our agent because he also lost a partner in that mission. His suspicions led him on an off-the-record manhunt. Thus the discovery of Collin's interest in the bones."

"So Collins probably wants them for their market value, especially since he seems to have contacts already established," she added.

"The FBI and the CIA have to make the bones disappear in order to prevent the natives from getting 'crazy'." Eric emphasized the word by making quotation marks in the air.

"Crazy?" she asked, wondering what he meant.

"We need to maintain status quo...statehood, U.S. property, etcetera."

"They don't want secession to gain a foothold," she said, realizing where he was going with his thought process. "So you're telling me the U.S. government, the HHF, *and* a couple of rogue agents are all after Cook's bones? So where does that leave me?" she asked.

"Since the U.S. wants the bones to disappear, and you want to take them to England, it only makes sense that we find them together to accomplish that. But once they're in England, they have to remain untraceable. Otherwise we haven't accomplished our mission."

"You mean your mission. My mission is to put them in their rightful burial place."

"Which is?"

"The same grave as his wife's in St. Andrew the Great at Cambridge Church. Since they were completely devoted to one another, it makes sense.

Besides, it's what my family would have wanted."

"If you do that, it will become public record."

"And if that happens, you think someone will dig them up," she said, shaking her head.

The slight nod of his head affirmed her own suspicion about what might happen if the bones were finally interred with Cook's wife. Since Nicole's ancestor's body had apparently never been surrendered to his men, and consequently his men unwittingly buried someone else at sea, what would prevent the HHF from stealing the bones again?

"We can't allow that. If we do, it could prove disastrous. We've discussed the perceived power of Cook's bones." he said.

"Gran told me the Hawaiians thought Cook sailed to earth from another dimension. She said they thought he was a superhuman ancestor. He befriended Chief Kalani'opu'u and by exchanging names and ritualistic regalia with the head chief, not only did he fuse himself to the most senior genealogical lines, but he also fused himself to the Hawaiian ancestor gods."

A furrowed brow etched itself across Eric's forehead.

Nicole continued. "The life-force of the gods was the chief's source of power, and his life-force transferred to others when he gave them his possessions, especially ritualistic cloaks and ornaments, and his name, like he did with Captain Cook," Nicole added.

"Which explains why it took four days for Cook's crew to get Cook's bones back," Eric said, studying her as she moved to the futon and dropped onto its fluffy floral cushion. Eric followed her lead and sat down, placing his left arm along the back edge. Close enough to touch her if she'd let him.

"*Thought* they got them back. Later, the Hawaiians told a Vancouver expedition member that Cook's bones were kept with Kalani'opu'u's bones at Hikiau Heiau across the bay from where the battle took place. They meant Kealakekua Bay. Kamehameha succeeded Kalani'opu'u as head chief, and the Hawaiians told an early European resident of Vava'u, Tonga that they kept Cook's bones as relics for ceremonial purposes," she said.

Eric frowned. "I vaguely recall reading something about that."

"The Hawaiian's declared they were still in possession of the bones. They said they held them in a place consecrated to a god, and every year they had a procession from that sacred place to other sacred places where they laid the bones on the ground and gave thanks to the gods for sending them such a great man," Nicole said.

"But didn't I read somewhere in the historical journals that the Hawaiians returned Cook's bones to Clerke, Cook's second in command, and he placed them in a wooden coffin and buried him at sea, with full military honors?" Eric asked, still frowning.

"Yes, but the only identifiable bones returned to the ship were Cook's hands, remember? He had a large scar on his right hand and the flesh was still attached." Nicole shuddered as she visualized this horror.

"So you're saying the rest of the bones could easily have been the remains of one of the four marines," Eric said, nodding.

"Especially since the Hawaiians dismembered them too. Cook's bones were sacred. The others weren't."

Eric's expression indicated he thought her logic was plausible. "I'll go with that," he said, resting his left ankle on the other knee, his right hand clasping it as he shifted closer to her. So immersed in the history of Captain Cook's demise, she didn't react to his smooth maneuver.

As if unaware, Nicole let her hand descend on his knee as she continued. "Then in 1823, a missionary visited the cave in the cliffs where the King had taken Cook's body from the beach, you know, before they gave someone else's bones to Cook's men. The natives told the missionary that Cook's bones remained in a temple with the priests, in a small wicker basket concealed with red feathers, but no one would tell the missionary exactly where this temple was."

With her hand still resting on his knee, Nicole could tell Eric's mind had begun to wander. If he knew what was best, he'd stay focused on this fascinating history lesson.

"And that's about the time the Hawaiians stopped parading the bones in the streets and they disappeared," she added.

"Until your parents apparently found them." He fingered a lock of her hair that had fallen on his left hand. "If we're not careful their demise might be ours."

"We won't let that happen," she said, her gaze locking with his. Compelling him to move closer.

"We can't afford to be distracted. We both know how dangerous it can be," he said.

She tried to ignore her impulse to plunge caution

into the depths of the sea. Her gaze intensified with inner desire. "I'm here to find the bones. So no, I don't have time for distractions. So in the morning, I'm going to the cliff."

"You have the most beautiful eyes," he said, leaning toward her as if he couldn't resist.

"You're changing the subject," she said, leaning back against his hand. Her eyelids closed as she inhaled, trying to escape the savage fire that threatened to consume her. "Life is too short."

He moved closer, caressing her forearm with gentle circular strokes. "Which is why it should be lived to the fullest," he whispered, his breath fanning her skin before he pressed his lips over hers.

At first, the kiss was light. Exploratory. Cautious.

But when she responded with all the repressed passion that exploded within, the kiss evolved into a volcano of ecstasy.

CHAPTER ELEVEN

"We should go," Eric's voice kept repeating.

Nicole rolled over and groaned. Why would anyone want to disrupt this delicious fantasy? But the persistent shaking of her shoulder served to jolt her back to reality, despite her subconscious objection, causing her lips to part with invitation at the hovering handsome face.

Damp hair indicated he'd been up long enough to shower, but the quick peck he placed on her lips didn't incite any passion, so she grabbed his neck and drew him down to press herself against his muscular frame.

The response was a brief linger. Long enough to ravish her lips with promise, but then he released her and rolled to the edge of the bed. "We should get going if we're going to search the Kealakekua cliffs without being observed."

Lace curtains didn't fully conceal the night sky. "But it's still dark."

"Exactly. We don't want to be seen."

She pushed herself up on one elbow and threw off the covers, heat flushing her skin as his gaze inched its way from her face down to her toes. "Well, I've just been seen," she said, grabbing her sarong off the floor, clutching it to her body as she dashed toward the bathroom.

A quick shower before leaving the cottage had refreshed her, aches and pains notwithstanding. In haste, she'd tugged on a pair of faded jeans, a red long-sleeved tee-shirt and a pair of red Keds. Protection from further exposure to sharp lava debris, and unexpected Kiawe on the cliff-side, was tantamount to the healing of her tender feet.

They parked Eric's Land Cruiser in the parking lot at Napoopoo Beach again, grabbed their backpacks and walked to the remains of the black lava rock platform of the Hikiau Heiau where Cook's bones had been kept so long ago.

"Every time I see a heiau it grieves me. The human sacrifices in the heiaus were made to appease the gods, but I can't even imagine," Nicole said in soft tones.

"I totally agree. It's as though the spirits of those sacrificed are still here," Eric said as he squatted down on his heels. His long-fingered hand brushed across his lips as he sighed. When he turned his gaze toward her, he paused momentarily.

"The history here is so moving, isn't it?" she asked.

Eric nodded in agreement. "We should get going, though. We still have a lot to accomplish."

They made their way to the edge of the heiau and pushed through the guava bushes, Palapalai and 'Ama'u ferns, picking up the faint cliff path that they recently had come down. Retracing their steps, stumbling occasionally in the dark on broken lava rocks and tufted grasses, Nicole thought, *this is a lot easier with proper footwear.*

Once they arrived at the crest of the cliff, Eric dropped his backpack and began rummaging through it for climbing gear. He handed her a compact walkie-talkie, a model she had become intimately acquainted with during her last mission in Africa. Her raised eyebrows implied the assumption that he'd borrowed company equipment without permission. His shrug seemed to confirm it.

"At least there aren't any horned beasts chasing you in the dark, Nikki."

"Thanks, Eric. That helps so much. And don't call me Nikki." When she turned away, the chuckle that meandered on the breeze caused her to shake her head.

After securing a woven climbing rope to a Hala tree at the top of the cliff, Eric wrapped it around a pulley, then around Nicole's waist. He placed a handful of clog stops and carabiners in her hand, silently watching as she clipped the clog stops to the carabiners before attaching them to her belt. Experienced at climbing, neither spoke a word as Eric followed suit with his own rope. Now Nicole knew why he'd been so well prepared when she fell over the edge of the rock wall two nights ago. Her hands still hurt beyond description, but accustomed as she was to ignoring pain, it shouldn't be a deterrent now. And as a fellow operative, she knew Eric wouldn't draw attention to her wounds, which both satisfied and irritated her. Sometimes she just wanted to be treated like a lady. With all the fragilities and delicacies bestowed upon her by a gentleman's consideration. But those feelings usually passed with such velocity, they weren't worth serious consideration in the first place. She wasn't that soft.

And now wasn't the time for passing fancies.

Before dropping down the cliff-side, Nicole flicked the switch on her headlamp to illuminate its LED bulb, sending eerie shadows into each opening of the cliff as she slowed to examine them one by one. The holes, caused by low-viscosity lava flows, made excellent hiding places. The hard crust that formed while the lava still flowed to the sea created numerous lava tubes in the cliff-side, making this treasure hunt quite challenging.

Disappointment surged time and again as she crept across the cliff-side like Spiderman. After moving all the way across her designated half of the cliff, she dropped a level, then another, then back to the center as the cliff revealed row after row of holes formed in the lava rock face. Most were so shallow her hand barely fit inside.

With little sleep, and lack of concentration due to the distractions of last night, she was about to call it quits. But before doing so, she decided to crawl across a section on the far right of the wall, toward the lush ferns that had overtaken the side of the hill and the edge of the cliff.

For some odd reason she felt compelled to survey the area. Perhaps Gran's spirit guided her.

∗ ∗ ∗

Dawn began to rise over the east side of the island as Eric began working his way across his designated half of the cliff-side. Nicole had disappeared from the rock face. And he couldn't see where her rope led. Rock and Hala trees and 'Ehaha and Hāpu'u fern camouflaged it. He tried reaching her on the walkie-talkie. After three attempts to establish contact, he decided something was wrong.

Fear rising in his gut, Eric inched his way across the cliff, so far to the right he thought he might run out of rope. It seemed like the wall ended. Hala and Ohi'a Lehua sprang up with such density only mangroves would be more difficult to traverse.

The surrounding ground cover of Palapalai and 'Ehaha fern had been disturbed, indicating something of interest had been recently explored. A cursory glance suggested more than one person had recently been there.

The hackles on the back of his neck rose, cautioning him to retreat.

Yet he pressed forward. How could he retreat without knowing where Nicole was?

He debated whether or not to use the walkie-talkie again. Most likely, his attempts to contact her a short while ago hadn't gone unnoticed. He had no proof. But he'd been trained to listen to his gut. And his gut told him someone had been listening. That same someone who had been tracking their every movement. That same someone who had followed them to the cottage from the bay two nights ago. That same someone who had also followed them to the cottage after dinner last night.

Someone wanted the bones as desperately as Nicole did. As desperately as Eric did, himself.

Which left him no choice. Follow his instincts. Nicole was in trouble.

With caution borne of years of exposure to danger, Eric pushed through the foliage. He only went a few feet before the vegetation stopped and the edge of a large black hole, a cave, began. The opening was about three feet by three feet, large enough to allow a man, or woman, to enter. Then he saw Nicole's rope snaking through the Hala trees, ending in a neat coil, hanging on nearby branches.

Eric poised at the entrance. He left his headlamp off, and stood still to listen, his feet gripping Hala branches below the entrance. Hearing nothing, he untied his climbing rope and looped it around Hala branches next to Nicole's, at the edge of the cave opening, which showed obvious signs of chiseling. Eric could see tool marks on the surface of the lava. Gathering his courage, he crawled into inky blackness.

The small entrance opened into a larger chamber high enough that he could upright himself while still on his knees. He couldn't see anything clearly, but sensed the chamber continued farther into the cliff. Outside, the sky had begun to lighten and he began to make out the sides of the chamber as his vision adjusted. There seemed to be crude carvings on the walls. Stick figures of humans? The back reaches of the cave were still cloaked in darkness.

Eric still couldn't hear anything. Should he turn on his light?

Something felt wrong. Instinctively, he knew Nicole had found what she'd been looking for. What they'd all been looking for.

Prudence was the better part of valor in most situations Eric found himself in. This was no exception. He withdrew a hunting knife from the belt clip on his right hip. The razor edge had been designed to slit the throat of a large animal...or man. His Colt .45 caliber pistol, while the most powerful weapon in his current arsenal, was too dangerous to wield inside such a narrow cavity of hardened lava. Besides, it lay buried at the bottom of his backpack, the barrel encased in a leather holster. Not exactly accessible while dangling from a climbing rope.

"Eric, are you there?" Nicole's voice startled him as it came across his walkie-talkie in a hushed tone. Still clutching his knife he grabbed the two-way transceiver and responded to the affirmative with a raspy whisper, betting both their lives he was wrong about someone listening in. "Where are you?"

"In the most amazing cave on the far right of the cliff."

"That's where I am."

"Then keep coming back. I'm not too far from the opening. Once you get all the way in, there's another small opening to the left. Go through it. I'm on the other side."

"Be there in a moment."

"And Eric," she hesitated, delight and sheer joy reflected in the soft nuances of her voice, "you'll be pleased with what I found. The search is over."

Her voice spurred him forward, despite the instinct that a perilous threat lurked just beyond the shadows. Yet, if Nicole sensed danger, she certainly wouldn't communicate over public radio waves. She would remain silent.

And he knew he could trust her instincts as much as he trusted his own. At least he hoped so.

He switched on his headlamp and continued

deeper into the cave. There were figures etched into the walls, but their symbolism only momentarily puzzled him.

When he pushed his way through the small opening Nicole described, what met his sight on the other side was nothing short of thrilling. Nicole sat on her heels with a look of sheer bliss on her beautiful features as she watched him shoulder his way through.

Encompassed in the circumference of light emitted from their headlamps lay a basket. Surrounding the basket were red feathers and a few ancient ornaments.

The basket revealed an assortment of old bones, including an intact skull, which was obviously Cook's, based on the size, the broad forehead and the high cheekbones. That, and a silver medal pinned to the side of the basket, lent authenticity to whose bones these were. Eric had read somewhere that the medal had been presented by Captain Cook to the native chiefs on his second voyage as evidence of the islands' discovery. They must have saved it along with his bones as a way of keeping that honor.

"How on earth did you find this place?" Eric asked, wide-eyed. Almost unconsciously, he removed the belt clip and slipped his knife into it before dropping it into his backpack.

"Over the years I've been on this cliff-side so many times I quit counting. This area always seemed like nothing more than a forest of Hala and 'Ōhi'a Lehua. I thought the caves and holes in the rock ended a hundred feet or so back. But last night, when we decided to head back to the cliffs, I figured there had to be some other place adjacent to Cook's monument besides the obvious ones. When I traversed to what I thought was the edge of the rock wall, for the first time I noticed a dark spot behind all the trees, so I decided to shove my way through the overgrowth and see what it was." She flashed him a smile reflecting her elation. "I can't believe we finally found it!" she exclaimed. Jumping into his open arms, she wrapped herself around him in a monkey hug, his nostrils flaring at the feminine scent of her.

He buried his face in her lustrous hair, inhaling until he felt lightheaded. His heart pounded at both the energy he'd expended to reach this place...and the awareness of impending danger. When she leaned back in his arms, she searched his face. "What?"

"Nothing," he said, tamping down the trepidation that would not evaporate. "This is incredible."

She slid to the ground, standing on her own two feet yet still hugging him, leaning back to study his expression. "You feel it too?"

"Feel what?" he asked, senses heightened.

"The danger." She released him, picked up the basket and stared at it for a brief moment. Her eyes filled with moisture. "My parents died over these." Then she drew a deep breath, as if to fortify herself, and swiped away the tears before pushing her way through the small opening, glancing over her shoulder, beckoning him to follow. "I don't think I'll sleep until we get these to the church at Cambridge."

"That makes two of us."

"As long as these are in our possession we're both risking our lives."

"Something with which we're both familiar."

"Something I'm willing to die for," she said.

"I'm not willing to die for them, but I am willing to

go to the limit for you."

"Eric, you don't have to do this. I'm quite capable of handling it on my own."

"And let you have all the fun without anyone to share the thrill of it? Besides, I've grown rather fond of having you around again," he said, giving her firm round bottom a pat. Falling in love with her again was more the truth.

If he were honest with himself he'd fallen in love with her the day he pulled her out of the wreckage in Africa -- her frail bruised and broken body lying limp in his arms as he vowed to get her out alive -- and that feeling had never gone away. But once this was over, she would banish him from her world. Which was bound to happen soon, since the bones were now in his possession. Loosely speaking.

They were both after the same thing, but for very different reasons. And those reasons would undoubtedly prevent him from ever finding happiness with this exciting, intoxicating woman.

Just short of the opening to the main cave chamber, Nicole halted. Eric bumped into her back, enjoying the jolt of her body against his. The silken blond ponytail swung from side to side, its fullness trapped in a yellow rubber-band, tickling his neck as she shook her head.

His body tensed.

With utmost care she squatted and set the basket on the ground. She turned toward him from the crouched position, her right forefinger pressed against her lips. She switched off her headlamp. Quickly, Eric switch off his headlamp. Nicole placed her hand on his forearm.

They were not alone.

Crouching behind her without making a sound, he slid the backpack off his shoulder and wedged it behind a huge lava rock jutting from the surface of the cave. He whispered in her ear, "Stay down. Don't move." She gave him a thumbs up. The warning was unnecessary.

It wasn't until that moment that Eric considered the only way out of the cave was the same way they entered. He moved slowly into the main chamber and could see daylight now streaming into the entrance. And the entrance was now blocked by an enormous shadow. "I see you leddin' da leedle woman carry you treashah basked."

Nicole had followed Eric into the main chamber and they now both rose slowly. Any quick movement would entice the man to use the weapon clutched in his beefy right hand, which would prove fatal.

"You cover been blowed, haoles. Not dat you ever had a cover, udder dan da dark a night." The Hawaiian man waved his left hand toward the opening of the cave. "Bud even dad canna help you now." A satanic smile spread over thick lips. "Ain' dad a bee-u-dee-ful Hawaiian sun-up?"

Eric knew better than to respond. Nicole's shallow breathing indicated she wouldn't say a word either.

But the Sig Sauer .357 clutched in the Hawaiian man's right meat-hook had them both wondering what the odds were on escaping with their lives. Not to mention the bones.

CHAPTER TWELVE

The large Hawaiian flicked a flashlight on and waved his weapon at Eric's head. "You so busy makeen love to dis beeuteeful woman you doan pay 'tention." He sneered. "Dat's why you led you gawd down. You doan nodeece tings." He pointed the light directly into Eric's eyes.

As the man moved in closer, the stench of sweat made Nicole nauseous. He laid the barrel of his handgun against her neck. Cold hard steel. Then he trailed it down her collarbone, stopping just above her left breast. "Bud I can see why."

In her line of work she'd become intimate with the feel of metal at her throat. But it still incited unmitigated rage.

And absolute terror.

She felt Eric's body tense behind her, as if he were the one with cold metal pressed against his pulsing flesh.

"Wha da madda? Wile pig godda you tongue?" His

laugh gave Nicole goose-bumps. Evil. Pure and simple.

"Puno, you got 'em?" Another heavy voice echoed through the cave.

The big Hawaiian man cocked his head to one side, waving his pistol in the air, providing Nicole with a moment to catch her breath. "Eee-yup. In hee-ah, man."

The other man entered the cave, his flinty gaze darting around the small lava-walled room. He, too, switched on a flashlight and illuminated the small opening to the back chamber where the bones had been hidden. Puno took a step back.

A red beam of light rested on the center of Nicole's chest. She shifted, but the Hawaiian men didn't seem to notice, as if they hadn't intended to actually aim the gun at her.

"Step aside, haoles," Puno said. He gestured toward the wall with the light. Nicole and Eric moved away from the entrance into the next chamber. The smaller of the men brushed past them. The odor of alcohol and sweat threatened Nicole's determination not to puke. The man kneeled down and reached one sweaty, brown arm into the back chamber.

Nicole recognized him. He was the same menacing man she'd encountered at the bay when she'd asked about the missing Hawaiian that had assisted her in launching her kayak. As the man lifted the wicker basket from its resting place, he grunted. Nicole caught the whiff of foul stomach gas permeating the air as the man rose. She remained stone-faced after feeling Eric's breath quicken.

Were they both losing it? Moments ago, she had a

laser beam blazoned on her chest, and now they felt like giggling? They were definitely losing it.

The man set the basket on the ground a few feet away, just inside the outer opening of the cave, then moved toward Nicole and Eric again. He withdrew a long switchblade from the front pocket of his grimy cargo shorts and flicked it open. After picking up a bag from the cave floor, he pulled out a length of clothesline and sliced a couple of two-foot sections from one end. Then he placed a filthy hand on Nicole's left shoulder and spun her around, making her stomach lurch. Now she faced Eric, and noticed the beam of red light had been trained on *his* chest. Her breath caught in her throat. The smaller man moved behind Eric, then tied and cinched the rope against Eric's wrists. Eric didn't utter a sound. After studying his handiwork for a brief moment, the man shuffled back toward Nicole and yanked her arms behind her. She clamped her eyelids shut as the nylon rope burned the flesh on her wrists.

She wanted to scream. It wasn't pain inducing the feeling, though. It was blinding rage. So close to succeeding with Cook's bones, the bones that were the reason for her parents' death. And now this.

"Sid down," Puno ordered in a deep voice from the shadows in the corner of the cave. He glanced at his cheap watch with his flashlight, then looked at his accomplice. "Lucille comin' when she dump da canoe."

Eric took two long strides toward Nicole and they lowered themselves back-to-back to the ground. He was thinking what she was thinking. Whoever Lucille was, it meant reinforcements were on the way.

"Stupeed lover," Puno sneered as he moved toward them. When they both looked up at him, he said, "Doan look so guildy. Whad I saw lass nighd...mmmmm." Then he shoved his gun barrel into Eric's shoulder. "An even doe you god da moves, Romeo, doan theen you can outsmart me. You untie ee-tha rope and you die." To emphasize his threat he placed the barrel of the handgun against Eric's chest and gave it a little shove. "Dat goes for you, doo, Julie-edd." He chuckled as he glanced at Nicole.

How many of them had been tailing them? And why hadn't either she or Eric noticed they'd been followed?

"You ready for a little celebration?" the smaller man asked Puno, causing the burly man to turn away from them. The smaller man held up two metal flasks.

Puno turned to him. "You stupeed eediod. We screw dis up and we dead," he said. "You wanna end up like da guy in da bay?" Then he waved a thumb at Eric. "You wanna led dis CIA boy ged da bone? You know he planneen on sendeen dem to da mainlan to make dem deesappear, you eediod. You realize da powah in dem tings? If da big Kahuna fine oud we had dem, and we too drunk to get dem to him, he have somebodee keell us. Jus like we did to da dummy in da bay. You gonna le dad happen?" The burly Hawaiian man's heavy footsteps echoed in the cave as he sauntered over and sat down on the ground beside the smaller man and leaned against the cave wall. "I doan tink so."

Puno's offhanded declarations about Eric's intentions pierced Nicole's heart. Every single concern she'd had regarding Eric's motives for helping her find the bones had just been validated by this murderer's statements.

Eric was after the bones, but to satisfy his own agenda. Not to help her get them to England.

This Hawaiian man and his side-kick intended to instill fear. She knew all the tactics. She'd even employed a few in the past to intimidate others. But the knowledge that Eric was working against her superseded all other emotion at that moment. The danger signals had been as clear as the water lapping the shore nearly two-hundred feet below, yet she was so busy diving into romance she hadn't recognized the danger signals for what they were.

The smaller man shrugged. "And if you keep your mouth shut for once, the big Kahuna will never know." Then he held up a silver flask and took a long swig. Very many of those and he'd be asleep on the ground in no time flat. Nicole could smell the stuff from across the cave. No wonder the man had gas.

This could work to their advantage.

But Eric was on his own now. No doubt he'd figure a way out without her help.

"You stupid eediot." Puno scooted closer to the smaller man. "Gimme dad ting." The smaller man passed the hammered silver flask and Puno took a couple of swigs, then swiped his mouth with the back of a dirt-caked sweaty hand.

Before long, between the two of them, they polished off the entire flask of what smelled like pure-grain alcohol. Then they began draining a second one, an indulgence that had already caused the smaller man to begin intermittent dozing. It was way too early in the morning for cirrhosis of the liver, but she was thankful these two had no such bias.

Eric apparently decided they were no longer a threat either, because he whispered, "I thought we ditched our tail last night. I should have known better. I didn't protect you, and for that I owe you."

Nicole twisted, pressing her left shoulder against Eric's right shoulder blade. The profile of his handsome features came into view as she twisted her head so she could see him. She whispered, "You never intended to help me get the bones to Cambridge did you? At what point did you decide to just sit back and let me lead you to them? After you seduced me?"

"Nikki, I..."

"Don't Nikki me. If we were anywhere else I'd forbid you to have any further contact with me. And I cannot believe these two slime-balls watched us. Makes me want to throw up." She turned and slammed her back against his. "And trust me, *that* will never happen again."

"I promise you these two will never watch anything we do again." He shifted a little, caressing her throbbing fingertips. "Things have changed since we were stranded near Cook's monument." He sighed. "After last night --" She curled her fingertips into fists. He continued, "-- but somehow I don't think what I say now will convince you of anything other than the conclusions you've drawn because of that man's comments." As he whispered he gave a nod in the direction of their two drunk captors. "All I can say is I'm sorry."

Heaving a sigh of her own, she whispered, "The only thing you're sorry about is that you got caught lying." She shifted. She tried to see his expression as she continued her interrogation. She also searched for some modicum of integrity in his face, praying she was mistaken in her assumptions, fearing she had indeed been duped. "Did you, or did you not intend to take the bones to the mainland and turn them over to the CIA?"

The expression that passed his features suggested he regretted failing her. "Yes, I was sent here to find the bones, no matter what it took."

"And what you took was me by saying you'd help me get the bones to Cambridge."

"I am a CIA operative. So are you. You know how this works. We honor our duty."

"I have a duty to honor, too. And it has nothing to do with the CIA."

"If the Hawaiian Hereditary Front gets the bones they will have enough power to cause an uprising that will only end in bloodshed. Perhaps even secession from the United States."

"It doesn't matter why. What matters is that you sold me out," she whispered, wretchedness reverberating in the accusation.

"I can see why you believe that. But since we're no longer in possession of the bones, the only thing that matters is that we get out of this alive. Neither one of us can afford to try fulfilling obligations right now."

When had he become like lava rock? Hard? Cold? Jagged?

"Whether we can or not doesn't discount the fact that you betrayed me. Those two goons over there know more about your character than I do. I should have known better than to give my hea -- than to trust you." A shudder of humiliation shot through her.

"You've given your heart to me? I'm humbled. I'll take it."

"I said my trust. My trust. Not my heart, Eric. And I'm rescinding it, since your character proves unworthy of anything I have to give."

"My character should not be in question. I am a man of honor and duty." He bumped her shoulders. "And it wasn't my imagination that you said you've given me your heart."

"Even if I did say it, we're nothing more than two outriggers passing on the surf," she said with sad awareness, no longer whispering. She meant nothing to him. Her throat tightened with suffocating heartache.

"Hey!" The burly Hawaiian man corked the flask and dropped it into the smaller man's lap, then heaved himself off the ground on knuckles large enough for a gorilla's hand. Nicole watched him lope across the small space until he stopped in front of Eric. He kicked the bottom of Erick's right foot. "You two love-birds...shud da hell up!"

Nicole sat in stillness, afraid to show any reaction whatsoever. But as the man turned away from them, Eric whispered, "Babe, when we get the bones back, I promise you we'll take them wherever you want. England, Africa, outer space. I don't care. And you have *my* heart too."

"I say shud da hell up!" Puno shouted, then grabbed Nicole's arm and dragged her a few feet away from Eric. Then he slammed the butt of his pistol against the back of Eric's head. Nicole watched in horror as Eric's upper body listed to the left before dropping to the ground. The force of the strike had rendered him unconscious.

Now she didn't have a choice. It was up to her to get them both out alive. She had no idea why the two men had been sitting around drinking instead of stealing the bones and disappearing. Waiting for reinforcements? How long would it be before reinforcements appeared?

Eric had a severe head injury now. He might even be dying. She didn't have time to wait for that to happen.

Desolate and bereft didn't begin to describe the overwhelming emotions that assaulted her mind at that moment. Yet she was a skilled CIA operative. She knew there had to be a way out. And despite the fact that Eric didn't deserve her adoration, her devotion, her love, she had no choice but to rescue him. Now all she had to do was put a plan of action into place.

But first she had to conceive a plan of action. Step one would be to get the ropes off her wrists.

With Eric's backpack laying a short distance away, hidden from their captors, she knew it contained the knife she needed to sever the rope. The challenge lay in preventing the two Hawaiian men from observing her actions. Otherwise she'd be unconscious too. Or worse.

For what seemed like an eternity, Nicole waited for Puno to join his light-weight partner in the drunken stupor that had overtaken him. Consuming the potent alcohol in the flask would render their captors helpless, giving her time to rescue Eric and get the bones to safety, as long as no one else appeared before she was able to get them out of there.

With every passing moment, Eric's situation became more grave. So when she finally heard snores bellowing from Puno, she figured it was safe to scoot to the backpack and unzip it a few inches at a time. Her hand brushed across something hard and smooth – Eric's knife! Her right hand closed over the textured handle as she rejoiced in silence. Lifting her head, she mouthed a thank-you toward the heavens, then began cutting through the rope binding her wrists. Employing a tiny sawing motion, her skin stung with each movement of the knife. Freedom seemed to take forever. When she finally cut through one side and freed herself, she then moved over to Eric and cut through his, too.

After throwing a quick glance at their captors to confirm their inability to prevent their escape, she rolled Eric onto his back, flipped on her flashlight and examined his head wound. A nasty knot had already begun rising from his skull. But to her great relief he didn't appear to be bleeding. At least not externally. She pressed hard on the knot with the palm of her left hand for a few moments, hoping to reduce the possibility of any long-term injury.

How she was going to get him out of this cave, and up the rock wall, would prove itself to be the greatest challenge of her skills and training. She stood there for a brief moment, then cut the section of rope still dangling from her left wrist that the smaller Hawaiian man had used to bind her wrists.

The durable climbing rope on the Hala branches outside the opening of the cave would hold considerable weight, since the rope was designed for all types of climbing. The only way she'd be able to get

Eric out would be to tie his body to hers, using her rope around their waists, and Eric's rope for reinforcement, once she got them out of the cave and through the trees.

As she shifted Eric to one side he moaned.

"Shhh...", she whispered. "We have to get out of here."

Without uttering another sound, Eric attempted to push himself up. Nicole slipped Eric's backpack over her shoulder and placed his arm around the back of her neck, then helped him rise to his feet. They tiptoed together toward the opening of the cave. She pointed to the ground. His body staggered forward. He caught his balance and lifted his arm from around her neck.

Determined to fulfill her promise to her grandmother at all costs, Nicole picked up the basket and set it down on the ground to Eric's left. Letting the backpack slip to the ground made it easier to grab the Colt .45 caliber pistol she'd felt inside the pack when she was searching for the knife. After verifying it was loaded, she slipped it into the waistband of her shorts. She retrieved their climbing ropes and pulled them into the cave entrance, then she tied Eric's around his waist and hers around her own waist, clipping them together with carabiners. Then she reached down and picked up the basket. Years of storage on the dry Kona-side of the island seemed to have protected the bones from deterioration, but the basket's weight and shape made it difficult to wedge between her body and Eric's, especially since he continued to fade in and out of consciousness.

Eric came to for a moment. She used hand signals to indicate they were about to move through the opening of the cave and up the cliff side. He grabbed the basket with his left arm and placed his right arm around Nicole and gave her a gentle squeeze of encouragement, then nodded his head indicating he was ready when she was.

A loud snort echoed through the cave. Nicole glanced back as Puno shifted from his spot where he'd been snoring.

When Puno stood up, inhaling a deep sniffling breath, Nicole reached behind her back and whispered, "Stay with me, Eric."

Puno let out a foul curse as he moved with lumbering drunkenness toward the mouth of the cave. Nicole's heart slammed against her breastbone. She grasped the Colt in her waistband and yanked it out. The hard cold metal clutched in her right hand felt heavy, but familiar. She hoped it wouldn't be necessary to fire it.

CHAPTER THIRTEEN

Agility seemed to be the huge man's secret weapon. Like a magician, a twelve-inch jagged-edged fishing knife suddenly appeared in his beefy paw. In one swift move, it rose high above his head, its tip pinched between the man's thumb and forefinger. His arm came down, but Nicole's training kicked in. As the knife sliced through the air, her forefinger squeezed the trigger of the .45. Burning heat seared through her hip as the knife struck her.

The bullet she fired plugged Puno dead center in the chest. The impact knocked his enormous body backwards against the cave wall. He staggered. When he finally fell to the cave floor, Nicole ignored the pain in her hip and quickly unclipped herself from Eric. She squatted and grasped Puno's feet. Pulling with all her strength caused everything to hurt, so she dropped his feet and began pushing and dragging him until he was at the edge of the opening. Puno groaned. Nicole jumped back. Then Puno rolled over at the mouth of the cave. Gravity took over. The large Hawaiian man plummeted into the Hala and Kiawe just beneath the cave entrance. Bright red blossomed on Puno's sweaty tank top. One beefy arm wedged itself between the branches of a Kiawe tree, suspending the pull of gravity for a brief moment. Then cracking sounds reverberated down the cliff-side as the branches snapped. Nicole clipped herself to Eric again. They shuffled toward the mouth of the cave and watched as Puno's lifeless body plunged into the sea below. Peering down, they could see blood-stained waves swirling below. Within moments, deadly crescent fins cut wakes toward the narcotic scent of blood. Tiger sharks would ensure Puno would disappear without a trace.

A wave of nausea flitted through Nicole's stomach before she shut down her emotions. Killing someone had never been easy. Even when she had no choice.

Warm blood trickled down her leg, reinforcing her own injury.

"Let's go, babe..." Eric whispered, "before the other guy wakes up, or that Lucille person shows up with reinforcements." His languid speech worried her as he gave her waist another weak squeeze of encouragement.

Rather than waste precious time tying up the smaller Hawaiian man lying there in a drunken stupor, she ignored him and clenched Eric closer to her so they could escape.

Edging their way through the 'Ehaha and Hāpu'u ferns and Hala trees almost proved her undoing. Her hip had only been grazed yet it burned like she'd sat on a lava vein. Eric's attempts at assistance between laps of consciousness made it more difficult than she'd imagined it could be. Finally, she glanced up at the most challenging bit and unclipped herself from him, keeping a tight grip on the end of his rope. Maneuver them both to the top edge of the cliff face would not be easy. She pulled herself up and stood for a moment, grimacing as she arched her back. Then she cinched Eric's rope around her waist and strained to pull him up and over the edge.

"C'mon, Eric. Help me!" Her muscles ached against his weight. Eric attempted to grasp the rocks as she pulled hand over hand until she though her arms would fall off. Finally, momentary relief enveloped her as his massive frame appeared over the top of the ledge. Once he was all the way up, Nicole sat down, sweating, and caught her breath. "We need to get out of here, Eric, before anyone else shows up."

Eric rolled over and looked up at her. "Sure, babe." Then he closed his eyes.

Nicole hauled him to his feet. She unclipped and untied both of their ropes, shouldered the pack, grabbed the basket of bones, and drew Eric's arm around her neck again, helping him back toward the faint trail leading down to Napoopoo Beach, and his awaiting car. She decided it was best to hike out instead of attempting to scale the wall again, despite the fact that she'd have to leave Eric alone with the bones while she hiked back to the car. No matter what, though, she'd have to wait until dark to do so. Or risk being spotted. And fired upon.

Two hours later, after several stops to listen for anyone following them, she finally rested in the thick of the Kāhili ginger. Eric continued fading in and out of consciousness. Nicole, exhausted and sweaty, was relieved that they were close to the heaiu, and the parking lot. After placing the basket within arms reach, she situated Eric in a small space between two Frangipani trees camouflaged by large lava rocks and administered first aid to her knife wound with supplies she found in Eric's well-stocked backpack. Eric's head lolled against her shoulder, so she shifted into a more comfortable position. While they sat, he mumbled about being in love, but she assumed that by the time a man reached his age he'd probably been unlucky at love once or twice, not counting their broken engagement, which was obviously not love. To be jilted, you had to have time to cultivate some semblance of a relationship. She'd only had time for work. And Gran. Now that both Gran and her work were gone there was nothing left.

As Nicole sat, her stomach reminded her that they hadn't eaten. Which meant lunch was still in Eric's backpack, and at the moment, she'd rather think about food than what happened back in the cave. Or broken engagements. Since Eric didn't seem aware of much of anything at the moment, she decided to eat one of the tuna snack packs he'd insisted on packing before dashing from the cottage in the wee hours of the morning.

The light lunch curbed her appetite. She took a long swig of water from a bottle she also found in the pack, then wet her fingertips with a little and touched Eric's lips. His eyes fluttered open. He reached for the bottle with urgency and took a long drink. She wondered when he would be alert enough to satisfy his growling stomach.

"Are we there yet?" Eric asked, grinning.

"I think we need to stay put until dark, Eric," she replied. "The HHF minions, and that includes that Lucille person, may be down here watching." Nicole thought if they left their hiding place too soon they might lose everything they'd worked for, everything they'd found. But if they didn't, Eric might suffer long-term effects from his head injury. And his eyelids were already fluttering closed again.

Eric would tell her to go with her instincts. She knew him well enough to know that. And her instincts told her he'd survive. He was made of tougher stuff than most men who'd been through the same training. He was the stuff heroes were made of, despite her personal disappointment in him a while back.

Her hands ached, especially the right one, which still bore strong reminders of the thorns from their first cliff-side adventure. Yet she felt compelled to slip it through his thick light-blonde hair until her body, mind and spirit could relax. With this constant heightened awareness, she hadn't realized how tense she had gotten. And as she relaxed, exhaustion overpowered her senses. The exhaustion felt overwhelming. She longed to give in and permit the lullaby of slumber to consume her, but she didn't dare. Instead, she shook off the sensation, shifted her torso and stretched her legs to keep herself awake. Her hip throbbed, as her hands had done earlier.

Late afternoon sunshine reflected contentment. Warm tropical breezes encompassed tranquility. Water lapping the lava rock nearby embodied peace.

When she woke, Eric was frowning at her. The fact that his pupils dilated properly buoyed her, though it was fairly dark, so she couldn't be sure he was okay. Even more disconcerting was that they were sitting in long shadows of moonlight as it played on the Hala and Frangipani branches shifting in the light tradewinds sweeping in off the ocean.

Anyone could have removed the basket while she slept, although she doubted they'd be able to take it without waking her, since her left arm still lay draped across the top. But still...

"You hungry?" she asked Eric. He didn't speak, but closed his eyes and nodded, so she reached in the backpack and withdrew the water bottle and another tuna lunch pack and opened it, mixing the tuna with the mayonnaise and sweet relish before adding a sprinkle of the pepper packet. She scooped the tuna onto a small butter cracker and handed it to him. He accepted it, shoving the entire thing into his mouth. Then she handed him water. He swigged a couple deep draughts, swiped the back of his long-fingered hand across his mouth and polished off the remainder of the tuna-laden butter crackers as fast as she could scoop the mixture on them.

"You got us out?" He winced another grimace. "I figured you would. I hate to ask, though. Do we still have the bones?" His speech had improved from the last time he'd spoken, which was encouraging.

In response, she patted the top of the basket with her left hand. "Yes and yes. Right here."

"You're amazing."

"You're half-conscious," she said, a trace of laughter in her voice. It was an enormous relief that his strength was returning. "I know this because your speech is still a little slurred and I'm not sure your pupils are dilating properly. You probably have brain damage."

"My brain is just fine. It's my legs that don't seem to want to cooperate," he said, proving his point by attempting to stand. His legs were like a newborn giraffe's.

"All you need is a little exercise."

"I hate to ask what you have in mind."

"How about a nice hike back to the car?" She beamed a smile at him through the soft moonlight.

"Fine. You carry the bones because the way I feel at the moment I'll scatter them across the ground and the basket will end up flattened underneath me," he said, staggering forward. "Lead on. I'll bring up the rear."

He flexed his legs one at a time then took a few tentative steps. "My head hurts like hell."

Laying a gentle hand on the back of his neck, the warmth of his skin sent a wave of adrenaline shooting up Nicole's arm. She snatched her hand away and let it fall to her side. Her face flushed with heat. "No doubt. You got clubbed with the butt of Puno's gun. I wonder what that name means in Hawaiian. Anyway, you were knocked silly with his gun, so I expect you'll still have a gnarly headache tomorrow," she said, grabbing the two headlamps out of Eric's backpack. She handed one to him, donned the other one herself, then tossed the backpack over her left shoulder and wrestled her right arm through the other strap so it sat securely in the center of her back.

"I should take that," Eric said.

"Put on your lamp and stop treating me like a helpless wahine. I might enjoy it so much I'll demand it in the future," she said, hiding the hope that he just might consider it.

His laughter sounded like full-bodied wine. Even half-conscious he could wield his magic over her.

To mask her feelings she bent down to retrieve the basket.

"I meant what I said back there, Nikki," he said while she had her back turned.

Bending over the basket, she took a deep breath, which was no easy feat while blood rushed to her head. When she stood she glanced up at him, half tempted to drown herself in his amber-green gaze. "And I meant what I said."

She began hiking through the guava bushes and Palapalai fern, the foliage slightly different and not as dense as it had been outside the cave, but still enough to provide adequate cover for the headlamps.

"We both know that's not what you want," he said after a moment of silence.

"We also both know why you're here." She shot a glance over her shoulder at him. "And why you started following me in the first place."

"I've already admitted to that offence. But I think the CIA will be satisfied with getting the bones to a location where the Hawaiian Hereditary Front can't find them, regardless of where that location is. That was my mission. Getting them to a safe place. They don't necessarily have to go back to the mainland."

"Oh, please. You know as well as I do they're going to demand absolute silence on this. They probably have someone following you too."

"I'd have noticed."

"I didn't notice you."

"Yes, you did. You just don't want to admit it."

"All I noticed is a smart-ass Flyboy who keeps showing up in random places."

"Like I said. You noticed."

"You think they'll trust *us* to know where the bones are? They're more likely to be paranoid that we'll divulge the location to a third party," Nicole said. "I doubt they'll trust us. It isn't how they work. They want the bones where they want them, not where I want them. They want them where no one knows their whereabouts, not where we have to dig up the center aisle of a church to place them in another person's grave. Even if it is Cook's wife's grave." She shook her head as she continued walking. "It'll be some top secret location, and only someone with black-ops clearance will have knowledge of the whereabouts of Cook's bones."

"Which qualifies us both."

She shrugged. "True, but --"

"Shhhhh!" Eric grabbed her forearm.

A gecko darted across the ground.

Eric continued to clutch her clammy skin.

The hackles on the back of her neck rose.

A cow lumbered across their path, staring at them as wide-eyed as Nicole stared at her.

"The wildlife on this island is going to be the death of me yet," she said, her right hand wringing the cotton tee-shirt draped across her fluttering chest.

"For a minute there --"

"Yeah, I know what you were thinking."

"I'm thinking I'd rather be sitting on a beautiful beach watching the sunset with you, sipping something stronger than water out of a plastic bottle, than limping through this god-forsaken brush in the dark, encountering stupid animals."

"If we get these bones to Cambridge, we'll do just that."

"Babe, you've got yourself a date."

Nicole grinned from ear to ear. The tattoo of her heart changed from one of fright to one of fancy. Even a stupid cow couldn't scare her at that moment. She had the promise of a bona fide romantic interlude with Eric North.

"So what happened in Africa?" he asked.

The question blindsided her for a moment. He'd turned the tables with his questioning, but if she could keep him alert she was willing to share inside information with him. After what they'd been through together, she knew she could trust him with her confidences.

Her steps slowed for a moment, then she picked up the pace again. "If we're going to get out of here before daybreak we'll have to step it up a bit. This okay?"

"Fine with me, as long as you answer my question and allow me to carry the basket," he said. She could hear his footsteps keeping time with hers, so she stopped and handed him the basket, grateful for the break. Her arms had begun to ache again.

"We'll switch off carrying it. It's a bit of a walk back to the Land Cruiser," she said, pointing in the general vicinity of the road where they'd left his vehicle.

"That's fine. What happened in Africa?" he asked again.

"It's a long story," she said, glancing back at him.

"I'm sure we have plenty of time."

They walked in silence for a few moments, forcing Nicole's mind to wrap around the sequence of events that culminated in the fatality of some of CIA's finest operatives. She stumbled on a sharp lava rock.

"It's the typical story. To gain as much knowledge as possible about the environment in which the military was operating, teams of social scientists had been sent in to act as military staff advisors. They were tasked with filling in the gaps in the military's cultural knowledge from a physical, social and religious standpoint."

"Right. That's common," he said, nodding in agreement.

"The Department of Defense had been scrambling to fix a crisis on a project they named Human Geo System. They were unexpectedly short-staffed when two entire teams of scientists had to be evacuated because of a sudden contagious and violent illness."

"Which is where you came in."

"My mission was to fly in one replacement team of scientists, then pick up the other. But rather than cancel the outbound flight when the scientists never showed up, my team was ordered to continue on without them."

"And that's what you were doing when your plane went down," he said in a gentle tone.

"We knew we were going to crash."

"I heard sabotage was the cause."

"I heard that too. Later. After I recovered from my injuries, and was placed on leave, there wasn't another whisper about it." Her footsteps faltered. "My partner was part of the crew. We were like sisters. We had worked together our entire careers."

"That must have been hard on you, Nikki." She could hear the sympathy in his voice. It soothed. And it grated.

"It's all part of the risk," she said. "She and I both knew it."

"It doesn't make it any easier."

"No, but it makes me more determined not to lose anyone else I care about to the cause."

"Meaning?" he asked.

"Meaning I couldn't leave you behind to let those two apes pummel you to death with the butts of their gun. I had no choice but to shoot that guy. I have to get those bones to Cambridge. And I've decided I'm leaving the CIA for good."

"And what career path do you intend to pursue?" he asked.

"I have no liquid assets, but Gran left me her house, so I could sell it and use the profit to start..." Nicole hesitated, then added, "Something. Don't laugh."

Eric did not laugh. "Do people like us ever really leave the CIA?" he asked.

"I plan to. And if they decide they'd rather shut me up than let me go, you're my witness." She grinned at him. "Just in case."

CHAPTER FOURTEEN

Rich laughter slipping from Eric's gorgeous mouth had an infectious effect. Hers soon blended with his in the soft warm breeze, but she wondered if she should be laughing or crying.

"What about you?" she asked. "I don't know much about you anymore, except you're a hot-shot pilot who rescues operatives from wreckages when there's no other means of escape."

"That about covers it."

"Oh, come on, Eric! There has to be more to you than that. Like where did you really grow up, how did you get involved with CIA and why? And why did they send *you* into the wreckage in Africa instead of someone else?"

"I was in the area. Just doing my job."

"I see. You never talked about this stuff before, either, but after what we've been through, you must feel a little like opening up now," she said, glancing over her shoulder as she maintained her pace. "What's your story, Flyboy?"

"It's really not as interesting as you must think it is."

"Boring works for me. It's a long walk."

"I'm sure you remember some of it."

"Humor me."

"If you insist. You might regret it."

"I said boring works for me right now. Get on with it."

"Fine. I was born in Michigan, grew up in the suburbs of Detroit. The only college I could get into was in downtown Detroit, so when we first started college, my cousin and I rented an apartment together. It was in the inner-city ghetto of Detroit." His voice hardened. "We weren't a family of means, and there were no scholarships. So we worked."

"The ghetto? Really? How awful." As Nicole reflected on her own college days, she worked hard, and her school wasn't ivy-league, but it was set in a wonderful smaller eastern town.

"As you can see, I managed to survive. Drugs, prostitution, and crime in general were all part of the scene. Things still haunt me. Back then, I wondered how I could stop the madness." His laugh was void of humor. "But what could a kid from a low-income family do to change the world?" He stopped walking. "Hell, I wasn't even sure I could change my own destiny."

"You okay?"

"You sure you want to go down memory lane with me?"

"We all have stories, Eric. Keep telling me yours. It'll help pass the time while we walk, if nothing else."

"Okay then. So after we finished college, my cousin and I decided to join the Air Force. Our intentions were less than honorable. We just wanted a way out. We were willing to do anything that would improve on the lives we had growing up. As officers, we had the opportunity to learn to fly, though, so we took it. Mark ended up in Iraq, flying secret missions. I decided to follow his lead and volunteered for anything and everything that might offer the thrill of adventure."

"That sounds honorable enough to me," Nicole said, shouldering low banana leaves aside as the trail became more and more overgrown. Her hip burned where the knife struck her, but at least the bleeding had stopped.

"One day a suit approached me and asked me to take a walk," he said with resignation, "and that's when I got involved in the CIA. I had seen things a person shouldn't see. So I thought the CIA would help me do my part to make the world a safer place.

"And that's how it all began."

"One thing led to another, and I ended up in Africa as your white knight. I have to say though, I was told it was a recovery mission, not a rescue mission."

Something akin to anguish swept over her. Memories of the incident were almost unbearable. "I almost wish it had been a recovery mission."

"You can't be serious. Look at all the fun you'd have missed out on if you had died there." His laugh this time was cheerful, as if he were attempting to lighten the burden she carried, the survivor guilt that consumed her at times.

"I'm sure you've been intimately acquainted with

that feeling," she said.

"Truth be told, it almost paralyzed me when my own parents died the same week my cousin's helicopter was hit by an RPG."

"RPG?"

"Rocket-propelled grenade. Have you forgotten what those are?"

"No, just thinking of your parents' death. Wow."

"I told you you'd regret hearing my boring story."

"Eric, I am so sorry." She turned and laid her palm on his forearm. "I shouldn't have --"

He shrugged, sloughing her hand off. "It was a long time ago. In our line of work, we can't afford to cling too long to our memories, or the emotions attached to them. It makes us weak, vulnerable, and dangerous."

"But your parents...and you and your cousin were like brothers." She stumbled again. "Just like the friendship I had with my partner."

"Grieving doesn't change the fact that they're gone. Our grief should propel us toward the greater cause more passionately. Which is why, once I felt the flicker of life in your body, your rescue became a personal quest for me in Africa."

"Thank you." It humbled her to know someone would risk his life to save hers. She had done it for others, but to have someone do it for her seemed to take on new meaning. Knowing it overwhelmed her.

He patted her bottom and said, "All in a day's work. And believe me, babe, you were worth it."

She stopped in her tracks, shook her head and rolled her eyes. "How do you do it?"

"What?"

"Manage to spin things so dynamically?"

"What are you talking about?"

"You turn every opportunity into an encounter."

"Opportunities shouldn't be wasted. Oh, look! We're just about to the Land Cruiser."

"My assessment of you is still accurate, even if you are trying to discount it by distracting me with the promise of a shower and comfortable bed." She laughed, trying to slough off the burden of everything that had happened to them. After all, they were still alive. And they still had the bones.

"Life is just one big exciting adventure. If a pretty lady like you is thrown into the mix, you'd better believe I'll enjoy it to the fullest."

"Like I said, you're a cad. How many other female ops have you hit on during your career?"

"Uh..."

She shook her head and waved her bandaged hand. "Never mind. I'd rather not know."

As they approached his SUV, he clasped her left hand. The intensity of his gaze filled her with unspoken promises. "Only you, babe, only you."

"Right. You've definitely got a head injury. Get in the vehicle." She opened the rear door, shrugged out of the backpack, took the basket from him and set it inside, then walked around to the driver's side. After sliding into the seat, she held out her bandaged right hand, palm up. "Keys?"

He waved his thumb toward the rear seat. "Front pocket of the backpack," he said, wedging his massive frame between the seats as he reached into the back seat. The keys dangled from his right forefinger when he leaned forward again. As she grabbed them, he planted a light kiss on her mouth, surprising her. Then he took her face between his strong, long-fingered hands and kissed her again. With meaning. With passion. With promise.

"We...uh...should --" she stammered.

"Do more of that?" Eric asked. She leaned away from him, hesitant.

After a brief pause, she settled into the driver's seat and fiddled with the keys. "Returning to the cottage isn't an option. Unless we want someone spying on us." She turned in her seat, risking an open gaze with the man she was in love with, hoping the cloak of darkness would mask her expression. "He hunted us. Tracked us like animals. And observed our...uh...most intimate moments."

"Trust me I won't let anything like that ever happen again," he said, regret and something else filling his amber-green gaze. "Let's get out of here. When you get to the top of the road turn right."

She put the key in the ignition. "Wait," she said, then turned and reached into the glove-box and extracted a Swiss Army knife.

"You're right. The headlights and taillights can't be turned off on this thing. Covering all the bases. Beauty and brains. So rare!"

Nicole shot him a quick glance and rolled her eyes as they got out of the vehicle and walked around to the rear. He watched her extract the slender screwdriver and remove the tail-light cover. Reaching into the shallow opening, she unscrewed the bulb. When she handed him the tool, he moved to the right and did the same thing to the right taillight.

"I'm not risking being followed again." She glanced

toward the sky. "Good thing the moon is out."

"You are still one smart lady," Eric said, juggling the small bulbs in his hand as he followed her to the front of the vehicle, opened the hood and unplugged the headlights one at a time.

After jumping back into the vehicle, Nicole turned over the ignition and headed out onto the road. When she turned right onto the main highway that looped the perimeter of the island she asked, "Where am I going?"

"We'll have to go to my place. As you pointed out, the cottage is the last place we want to be. It's no longer safe."

Neither would she be safe at Eric's house, should her feelings betray her. He'd said things that implied they had a future together after all, but she wasn't sure if he had any feelings of depth, or if she'd get kicked to the curb again. Lust could be the overriding emotion here, and she'd better pay attention this time.

For her it was love. Plain and simple. It always had been. And that was her problem.

Eric's house was a plain square structure on a narrow strip of fenced land, enveloped in eucalyptus, breadfruit trees, Koli'i, and other endemic and native Hawaiian foliage, so dense it seemed cut off from civilization, reminding her of the cottage's appeal. As she pulled into the drive, he instructed her to park around back where the gravel ended just shy of a small cement pad hosting two Adirondack chairs and a wood-burning fire-pit. The crashing surf sounded a short distance away, muffling the energy of nature, but she knew when the sun rose it would be visible from this vantage point on the hillside.

Eric grabbed the basket of bones from his side of the SUV. Nicole retrieved the backpack and slung it over her left shoulder.

Inside, the house was small. Eric had furnished it with heavy dark brown rattan furniture upholstered in dark-green leaf-patterned fabric, suitable for a bachelor. He set the basket down on the snack bar just inside the entry door, then lifted the backpack off her shoulder, placing it beside the basket.

He turned toward her, his hand still resting on the backpack. "I haven't thanked you properly for getting us out alive," Eric said, his gaze reflecting a glint of wonder as he stood just inside the kitchen. "You're one amazing lady."

"As someone once said, all in a day's work." She cleared her throat, attempting to dislodge the lump created by the nerves dancing in her belly. "The sun will be up soon. We should get some rest," she said.

Awkwardness hung in the air like a dense curtain of fog. Until Eric swept her into the circle of his brawny arms. The roughness of his embrace suggested emotion so tumultuous that he could only camouflage it by burying his face in her neck. His left hand stroked her hair. He whispered, "I thank you, and the CIA thanks you."

"*You're* welcome," she whispered back, tears springing to her eyes. "But the CIA is *not.*"

His embrace tightened.

Throwing her arms around him felt natural, as if his body represented the tower of strength she'd been searching for all her life, but didn't know it. She'd never felt quite this sure about him until now.

They stood in each other's embrace without a word

passing between them, yet she felt a deepening desire enveloping them both.

She composed herself before Eric noticed her tears. His right hand moved up her back drawing sensuous circles across her shoulders while his left arm remained tight around her waist, pressing himself against the length of her. The nerves dancing in her belly now balled together to form a knot in her stomach, which began pulsing like a heartbeat.

The gentle stroking of his right hand transitioned to a soft caress on her neck as his fingertips brushed the hair aside. His warm lips seared a path of persuasive surrender along her neck, his light breath on her skin fanning the heat flashing throughout her body.

Already feeling drugged, she moaned in anticipation of what was to come when his lips possessed hers.

Abandonment of her sanity ignited an explosion of fiery passion designed to suspend all else until sheer exhaustion tugged them back to reality.

Later, as she lay in the dawn of the morning, listening to the chorus of birds outside the window with Eric's left arm resting across her stomach, Nicole resolved to take one day at a time. What happened after the bones had been entombed would happen as fate would have it. The delicate threads that wove them together remained as fragile as the coral reef in the waters surrounding Captain Cook's monument.

Nothing felt certain. Nothing had been declared. Nothing had been promised.

Except a romantic sunset on a Hawaiian beach.

With the passing of everyone she'd loved in her

lifetime, she'd begun to close off her emotions. Now she resolved to love someone without knowing if she was loved in return. Someone who had lost everything, too. Someone who thought emotions should be used as a propeller.

He was flirtatious. And passionate. But he held himself in check, as if he feared his emotions would engulf him.

For self-preservation she would operate under the assumption that she was nothing more to him than a distraction created by a mission he'd been sent on. He'd even admitted as much back in the cave. Declaring love in the heat of the moment never rung true. They were three meaningless words spoken together in spontaneity. He did say, though, that she had his heart when they were in the cave. But what did that even mean to him?

It was all she had hold on to, though, she thought as she drifted into restless sleep.

In her dream, she felt the trade-winds brush across her bare shoulders and shuddered. Fighting fear in the misty reality of her dream, she heard Eric's whispered voice say, "I kept the basket so she doesn't suspect anything. Take this package and get out of here before she wakes up. We'll connect in England." In her dream, fear paralyzed her.

Thrashing in her sleep, her legs tangled with the sheets, fueling her misty dream-like fear, tipping her into a full-fledged nightmare.

Both men standing in the entry-way of Eric's house ceased movement. Hearing Nicole thrashing in the bedroom, Eric wordlessly signaled for the other man to disappear. The man tucked the package under his arm and within a split second disappeared into the early morning dawn without a trace.

Eric tiptoed back to the bedroom and crept into bed, then gathered Nicole into his arms. She felt damp with perspiration. He soothed her into more peaceful slumber again, murmuring sweet nothings against her brow, feeling a deep satisfaction that Cook's bones were in trustworthy hands. Nicole would feel double-crossed if she knew what he had done, but that thought was not to be entertained at that moment. Time enough in the morning to figure out how to pacify her, should the need arise. For now, all he felt was relief. And gratitude for his CIA contact.

CHAPTER FIFTEEN

Warm sunlight blazed across the bed when Nicole woke. Judging by the sound of water rushing though the pipes in the adjoining wall, Eric was already in the shower. Without clean clothes, she would shower and dress in what she'd worn all night, unless she could convince Eric to return to the cottage for her things.

When she broached the subject over a light breakfast of bananas, guava, toast and scrumptious Kona-grown coffee, he agreed they should collect her belongings.

He raised his chin toward the door. "As you can see I'm already packed. As soon as we pick up your things, we'll leave for Honolulu on the next available flight. The sooner we get the bones to England, the better off we'll both be. Hopefully, the drunk Hawaiian hasn't reported back to his Kahuna. Since the big burly guy became shark food, and the smaller man doesn't have Cook's bones, I'm counting on the fact that he's afraid to make contact with his boss.

Because if I'm wrong, we'll be lucky to get off this island with our lives."

"And you're one-hundred percent on board with taking the bones to England, right? You're not going to double-cross me when I'm not looking?" she asked, desperate for his partnership in getting the bones to where they belonged.

"If you don't trust me by now, the future will be more challenging than I can handle."

"I trust you. But I need reassurance right now."

"After this morning?"

"Especially after this morning. Let's face it Eric. You're not exactly a family man. You're more like a love-'em-and-kick-'em-to-the-curb kind of man. You haven't exactly instilled a lot of trust in me."

"Trust me. I did not hold back this morning."

"You know what I mean."

"I'm one-hundred percent onboard," he said, waving her off in obvious frustration as he went out the front door.

The bones would get to England. How they got there was out of her hands, but somehow he'd made her feel less reassured than ever.

The Land Cruiser's engine sat idling when Nicole opened the front door. Eric sat in the driver's seat tapping his fingers on the steering wheel. She glanced back at the snack bar. Since the basket with the bones was no longer there, she assumed he'd collected them, and all she had to do was join him in the SUV, so she turned the lock in the front door and pulled it shut behind her, testing the knob to ensure it was latched and locked. His expression was shuttered as she hopped in the vehicle, confirming her assumption that she'd offended him.

Once they stopped at the cottage and she'd packed her small suitcase, she phoned the airline to check on available flights to Honolulu, with connections to Heathrow. A flight was scheduled to depart Kona in two hours with a connection to Heathrow an hour after arrival in Honolulu, so she purchased two seats all the way to Heathrow with the credit card Eric handed her. It dawned on her that her suitcase contained no appropriate clothing for London's cooler climate, and there wouldn't be time enough to stop at her apartment in Honolulu, so she'd have to make do with what she had in her carry-on, and figure out later how to reimburse Eric for her airplane ticket. She didn't want to owe him anything

*   *   *

As they headed to the airport, Eric made a show of stopping at a shopping center to purchase a box, bubble wrap to protect the basket during transport, and a roll of packing tape. The short drive to the airport was accomplished in uneasy silence, but it wasn't for the reasons Nicole thought it should be.

All she needed was reassurance.

Once inside a parking spot at the airport lot, Eric shut off the ignition and exited the vehicle, all accomplished with an unspoken demonstration of his displeasure.

He wrapped and sealed the basket inside the box and slapped the top of the box. "Write your name on this," he said, thrusting a black Sharpie in her direction. "That should prove *something* to you."

"I didn't mean to upset you," she said, adjusting the hem of her coral tank top as she glanced at him.

His dark expression confirmed her suspicions.

"No worries."

She placed a hand on his forearm. "I really am sorry, Eric."

He averted his gaze, so she took the thick marker from his open palm and wrote her name in large block letters on the top of the box. As soon as she finished, he reached into the backseat and yanked his rolling suitcase out of the vehicle, then jerked up on the black extension handle hard enough to yank it completely out of the top of the suitcase. With pursed lips, he reached in again and slid the box to the edge of the seat, then wrapped an arm around it and hiked it onto his hip. "I'm going to the ticket counter. Since we share one confirmation number, perhaps you should join me."

"Eric, I said I was sorry. There's no need to treat me like this."

He paused, turning toward her. "Let's get one thing straight. I will help you get the damn bones buried in the location of your choosing." His expression reminded her of hurricane clouds blowing in without warning. "Got it?"

"Loud and clear," she said. She wasn't sure whether she should be relieved or even more concerned.

"Good. Let's go," he said, heading toward the ticket counter with lighting speed.

When it was finally their turn at the counter, the agent measured the box then gave Eric a sympathetic smile. "I'm sorry sir," she said, "but this box will have to be checked. It's simply too large to fit in the overhead bins, or under the seat. It exceeds the height and width requirements for our small overhead bins."

"Check it?" Nicole asked. "Uh --" Nicole looked at Eric, panic setting in with a vengeance. "But --"

"It's no problem. You can insure it miss," the young agent said, smiling again with all the charm she'd clearly been trained to use with difficult travelers.

Nicole had to trust the airlines to get her ancestor's bones all the way to Cambridge? How could she trust absolute strangers when she wasn't even certain she could trust the man standing right beside her?

The gardenia blossom secured in the pretty agent's hair had such a heady fragrance that it transported Nicole back to the cottage for a fleeting moment. A fleeting moment that afforded her the opportunity to wrap her head around this latest challenge.

She couldn't be this close to satisfying a deathbed promise to Gran and risk losing the bones now to an entity that had absolutely no interest in their value. She'd rather lose them to the CIA than have the airlines ship them to some obscure location to rot on a conveyor belt in Timbuktu.

"Do you trust me?" Eric asked her, his gaze implying their entire future rested on her reply.

"I...uh --" Nicole feared the toast and fruit she'd eaten earlier would end up in vile chunks on his tan loafers.

Eric closed his eyes and shook his head. He looked at the agent and said, "Please insure it for a million dollars."

"A million dollars? Well sir, you'll have to declare the contents of the box and validate its worth before I can insure it for that amount. Plus, it'll cost extra," she said, fumbling around in a drawer behind the counter for the necessary paperwork.

Eric reached in his pocket and withdrew his wallet, pulled out his government ID and placed it on the counter, two long fingers pinning it to the smooth surface. Then he slid it toward the agent, rested his forearm on the counter and leaned in, his eyes narrowing with sultry secrecy calculated to make the poor woman buckle. "This box contains government property. It is irreplaceable. And I'm going to need your cooperation in getting it to Honolulu --" he paused, glanced at her name badge and continued, "-- Grace." The smile he flashed her would have collapsed kingdoms, were they ruled and occupied by female royalty.

"Well sir, this is highly unusual. I'd love to help you, but I'll have to speak to my supervisor first," she gushed.

"Grace, I'm sure you can appreciate the fact that this is a top secret matter. If we bring your supervisor in, it will no longer be secret. You look like a woman of great intelligence. You can imagine what kind of risk I'd be taking by involving anyone else." He paused. "Besides yourself, that is."

The young pretty Hawaiian woman hesitated, chewing on her lower lip with large pearly-white teeth. Then she flashed Eric a sweet smile and said, "Well sir, if I may say so, my supervisor is very trustworthy. She'll record the information and lock it away."

"I can appreciate that Grace, but *my* supervisor is a vicious lunatic who will rip my head off if he finds out anything about this transaction was documented."

"Oh, sir. That's horrible." She hesitated, then glanced across at the customer service agent standing at the next counter. "I suppose I could simply insure it, and we could say museum artifacts on the document."

"Your name suits you. You are a woman of grace and generosity. I would kiss you if this massive counter wasn't between us."

As if mesmerized by Eric's flirtatious abilities, a slow fiery flush swept across Grace's petite face. The poor woman must have had sweat running down her spine with the heat of it.

"Well sir, delightful as that may be, that's not necessary."

Eric leaned forward causing Nicole to believe for a brief moment that he actually intended to kiss the woman. Then she watched his lips move as he whispered, "I am forever indebted to you, and if it were possible, the CIA would thank you. I'll see to it that this doesn't go unnoticed with your supervisor."

"Oh, sir! Please don't say anything! I'll get fired for ignoring the rules!"

Eric pressed his right forefinger to his lips and nodded. "Point taken," he whispered.

Nicole remained in a state of admiration as they boarded their flight to Honolulu. She'd been known to pull out all the stops when faced with roadblocks, but she had never stooped to actually using the CIA and flirtation to get what she needed, unless it was actually for official government business, but then never flirtation. She wasn't sure if she should be appalled, or impressed by Eric's increasingly unique tactics. He was a dichotomy of professionalism and rakishness.

Throughout the flights, and the intervening time in between, Nicole thought of nothing but the bones.

The box Eric had sealed them in was nondescript, which was the best disguise possible. But if anyone observed the progress of the bones from the cave to the Kona International Airport, they were still at risk of being stolen again. In fact, every checked item was subject to any number of mishaps. Misdirection. Loss. Theft. Damage. Destruction.

The thought of all the uncontrollable possibilities made the dull foreboding ache at the back of Nicole's brain rise to the forefront.

Any one of those situations would halt her ability to fulfill her promise. And sharing her fears with Eric would only cement them. Besides, she figured his thoughts ran along the same path.

Many hours later, at Heathrow Airport, exhausted and nervous, Nicole made her way to baggage claim in silence, alongside Eric, who seemed surprisingly calm, considering the situation. She almost collapsed when the conveyor belt began spewing its load onto the rotating carousel at the bottom of the chute. The first item down was the box.

Undamaged.

Eric pressed through the crush of people and snatched it, his sensual lips curving into a satisfied smile as he approached her.

"Now we have customs to deal with," he whispered in her ear as they moved toward the queue to exit the international arrivals terminal.

"I'm sure you have something up your sleeve for that too," she whispered back. His eyes crinkled in amusement, causing her to release some of her pent-up tension with a delicate laugh.

"I plan on stating the truth. It's how we filled out

the insurance and customs forms. Too risky otherwise," he said in low tones. "Museum artifacts."

As they approached the customs counter Nicole's nerves were humming. Would this be where the mission ended? Would customs confiscate the box? Would this nightmare ever end?

When Eric moved through customs without more than a brief question about the purpose of his trip she was stunned. Her own interrogation had been more stringent. What was she bringing into the country, how long was she staying, where was she staying, with whom was she traveling?

He waited at the exit while she caught up with him, a look of utter confidence splayed across his features.

"How did you get through that so easily?" she asked, grabbing his shirtsleeve.

He thumbed toward the customs agent who had just quizzed her and said, "I said I had nothing to declare."

"But it's a huge box!"

"Which I said was clothes I was donating."

"That doesn't even seem ethical." This man was in a whole different league.

"Do you trust me now?" he asked, amusement lingering in his beautiful amber-green eyes.

"I...you're --" Her voice faded.

"I know. I'm amazing," he said, still smiling as they passed through the automatic glass doors and out into the watery sunshine. He glanced down at her, eyes twinkling. "Tell me you trust me."

"It hasn't been easy, but okay. I trust you." The admission was dredged from logic and reason. She realized then she could have trusted him all along.

The cab driver attempted to take the box from Eric and put it in the boot of his auto, but Eric clutched it, insisting it ride up front with them. The driver shrugged his shoulders, then slammed the boot shut and hopped into the driver's seat. He glanced in the rear view mirror and asked where to, and when Eric rattled off an address in London, Nicole looked at him with suspicion.

He glanced at her, then directed his gaze through the front windshield. "My place," he said.

"We need to go to Cambridge," she said. Then she tilted her head and frowned. "Just how many places do you have?" she asked. Obviously he had done better than she had at investing his income.

"I keep a modest apartment here because I'm here so often," he said, slipping an arm along the back of the seat. He leaned toward her and inhaled.

She cocked her head at him. "Focus, Eric. We need to go to St. Andrews in Cambridge first."

"With a jackhammer and a shovel?" His laughter irritated her.

"We need to scope it out."

"We need to freshen up first. Then I'll make a few calls and we'll grab another cab."

"I forgot. You have people. And are your people going to 'bury' the bones for us, too?"

Without a doubt, he had connections. Connections she probably wasn't even aware of. And most likely, one of those connections was inside the church of St. Andrew the Great at Cambridge. Nothing would surprise her at this point.

His apartment was indeed modest. A tiny studio overlooking a dingy courtyard in the middle of a busy street in Hampstead. It was a far cry from his house in Hawai'i. Still, it afforded a place to shower. Nicole wasn't above modest living herself. Her own place in the outskirts of Honolulu was even more humble than this place.

While she showered, she could hear his deep voice conversing with someone, but she couldn't make out what he was saying. It was probably safe to assume he was making arrangements for their visit to the church, perhaps even getting permission to bury the bones this very day.

What a relief that would be!

But then it was late, so perhaps that wasn't possible today.

As Eric stepped into the shower, she towel-dried her hair and glanced at the box setting on a narrow table barely large enough for two dinner plates. Elementary lettering on the top of the box lifted the corners of her mouth with amusement.

But the tape across the top was three layers thick.

She leaned her head against the doorjamb and asked, "How many times did you run tape across the top of the box?"

The sound of Eric briskly rubbing his skin with his hands made heat rush to her face. The scent of his soap took her back to the islands again for a fleeting second.

"Twice. Why do you ask?"

"There are three pieces of packing tape on it now."

"It's been opened?"

"Maybe. Someone clever enough could have opened it then re-taped it, hoping no one would notice. It has three strips of tape now instead of two."

"Open it. I'll be out in a sec."

Nicole's heart pounded as she retrieved a paring knife from one of three small kitchen drawers. With it poised over the box for a brief moment, her heart raced.

When Eric entered the room with a towel cinched around his muscular hips, Nicole sucked in her breath, completely forgetting what she was about to do.

"Go ahead," he said, nodding toward the box, obviously unaware of what the sight of him and his naked torso had done to her ability to remember what she was doing.

Eric removed the knife from her hands and in one swift move sliced it open. The breath Nicole had sucked in a moment earlier now escaped her lips.

The contents of the box was not what she expected. Smooth rocks of various sizes, weighing approximately what Cook's bones weighed, about thirty pounds, was what she saw.

"*Oh, NO!*" Nicole screeched.

Eric grabbed her by the upper arms and bent down so he was eye to eye with her. "Calm down! The bones weren't shipped in this box," he said in a soft voice. "I knew they'd never make it through customs, not to mention that just about everyone who is after them would have had ample opportunity to take them if we had transported them as checked baggage. The fact that someone *had* tampered with the box means that I made the right decision to get the bones to England through the CIA, not by trying to transport them ourselves."

Her gaze grew wide as she sucked in a deep breath. "You *lied* to me," she whispered as she tore herself out of his grip.

"I said you could trust me to get the bones back to England. That was not a lie." At her gaping mouth, he continued. "They are waiting for us with my contact at Grosvenor Square."

"The American Embassy in London," she said, her gaze narrowing in disgust. "You used the CIA."

His gaze narrowed, too. "Babe, I *am* the CIA."

"I'd better get the bones back," she said as she turned away from him, feeling like she had been kicked in the gut. This confirmed two things in her mind. He neither loved her, nor was he to be trusted. If the bones disappeared again, she would have no way to continue the search. All her resources would have been exhausted, not to mention her body and soul. And all for naught. At this low point, she had no choice but to stick to Eric like sap oozing from a dying pine tree. Which is exactly how she felt.

How could she have been so naïve?

The hook was Cook. And she let her search for his bones hook her. It had become an obsession that might just lead to complete and utter failure.

CHAPTER SIXTEEN

Eric knew he had risked a future with Nicole by handing off Cook's bones to a trusted contact. He also knew it was the only way the bones would make it safely to England. It was a calculated risk that he had no choice in making.

"I have the package," the voice on the other end of the cell phone said in his ear.

Eric nodded as he spoke. "Good. What time and where?"

"One hour at The Barley Mow. Near enough to the Marriott to provide some distraction."

"And near enough to the Embassy to provide a place of escape should we need it." Eric nodded again, glancing at Nicole's angry gaze.

"If you're not there in one hour, I will disappear and we'll connect later."

"Likewise," Eric agreed before ending the call.

"So now what?" Nicole asked.

"Now we meet my contact who will give us the

bones. Then we can take them to the church, as planned."

Nicole shook her head. "If one thing goes wrong, that's it. We're finished." That comment gave Eric a modicum of hope that she hadn't already completely written him off.

Hailing another cab wasn't difficult, and within minutes they were headed toward the pub. Eric wasn't taking any chances on being late. He figured they could sit at the pub and have a soda while they waited for his contact to show. Not that he wanted to hang around anywhere waiting for a contact, but in this situation he didn't have much choice. Getting the bones took precedence over any other concerns. He would not let Nicole down.

"We'll get out here," Eric said to the cabbie, as he held a large bill folded longwise between his first and middle fingers so the cab driver could see it. The cab driver took the cash as the cab came to a quick stop on the corner. With one hand on the door handle and the other grabbing Nicole's hand, Eric opened the door and the two of them practically leaped out of the cab. While focused on his destination, Eric was still acutely aware of their surroundings, absorbing every detail. When Nicole tugged on his arm, he glanced at her, trying not to let her see that her distraction might be dangerous.

"Eric!" She slowed, forcing him to take smaller steps, too.

"What? Are you having trouble keeping up?"

"Eric, isn't that Collins?" She nodded her head toward the doorway of William Hill.

"Where? I don't see anyone that resembles him."

She shook her head. "Maybe I'm seeing things. I swear it was him, though. He was right there in the doorway, now he's gone. Perhaps it was someone who looked like him."

"They say everyone has a twin somewhere in the world. I would have seen him if he was really there. Your nerves are fried, making you imagine things. Once we get the bones to their final resting place, we can both relax and stop imagining things."

Nicole's laugh held no mirth. Her nerves were as taut as a band of steel supporting London's Tower Bridge.

"Here we are," he said, as he opened the door, holding it for her to enter ahead of him. His eyes slowly adjusted to the dim lighting inside. The place smelled of beer and fried fish. A quick surveillance of the bar told him they arrived before his contact. Eric glanced at his watch. It was just mere minutes ahead of their scheduled meeting time. Not the most ideal situation, but it was better if they arrived ahead of his contact, so the other man wasn't a target. The least exposure possible ensured the best protection of his contact's identity.

Choosing a table in a back corner, where Eric could see the sidewalk leading to the main entrance, he was taken by surprise when ex-CIA agent Doyle slipped into the bench seat alongside him at the same time the waitress came to the table. She glanced at all three of them and said, "How about a drink?"

Shaken by the sudden and unexpected appearance of his former partner, Eric's eyes narrowed and he said, "Can you come back in a few minutes?"

The waitress smiled and said, "Just let me know

when you're ready," and sashayed away.

"Hey Eric, long time, eh?" Doyle asked, his beady-eyed gaze locked with Eric's.

Eric's stomach lurched. Although it was fleeting, the expression on Nicole's face was one of alarm, something akin to what Eric was feeling himself.

"What are you doing here?" Eric asked the new arrival, knowing the answer was not going to be one he wanted to hear.

"A little birdie told me *you* were gonna be here."

"What little birdie?" Eric asked, dread filling his mind.

"Eric, really!" The other man sneered. "I still have my contacts on the inside. You, of all people, should know that."

"What do you want?"

"I know somebody who wants your package – someone who will pay big bucks for it. He's Chinese, so it will disappear and no one will know what happened to it." The satisfied smirk made Eric's fist twitch, but he decided against letting it punch Doyle's evil face.

"What package?"

"Can't you see you're interrupting a date, mister?" Nicole broke in, fully aware now who this man was, and what he wanted.

"Sorry, lady, but that simply won't do. I know why you're here. And since you won't cooperate, I guess I won't either." As he rose from the table, he gave them both a cursory glance through narrowed eyelids, coupled with a wicked smile. "See ya around," he said with a light tap on the tabletop, and then winked at Nicole before disappearing around the corner where the restrooms were located.

"Damn!" Eric jumped up and ran toward the restrooms, mentally kicking himself for not checking the place out as he normally would have.

An agonizing groan escaped Eric's lips. Face down, eyes open, laying in a small pool of blood from the bullet hole in his neck, lay his contact. And the bones were gone.

At his elbow, Nicole quickly assessed the situation, "Come on, Eric. There's nothing we can do for him now except let your handler know."

Eric hesitated. "I could have prevented that."

"How?"

"I should have checked the premises."

"It could have been you."

"No. He wouldn't have shot me."

"How do you know? I'm assuming that was Doyle, wasn't it, who did this?"

"Yes."

"We need to go, Eric, before the bones disappear forever. I'm assuming Doyle's working for himself these days. Either that, or he's gotten in way over his head with the wrong people."

Eric shook his head as if to clear his mind. "Where the hell did he go?" he asked as they ran out the back door.

Nicole pointed to a Mini with darkened windows picking up speed as it passed in front of them. "And I swear Collins was driving."

When Eric's forward momentum came to a halt, Nicole plowed into his back, almost falling down as she collided with his solid frame. Eric grabbed her by the arm to steady her, and glanced at his watch again.

"Damn it! Come on. I knew something wasn't right. And now I get to explain this latest development to my boss." With his hand still on her arm, he started running toward the street, hailing a cab that had conveniently been sitting there.

Yanking open the door, Eric shoved Nicole inside and shouted, "Quick, follow that car," while he still had one foot on the sidewalk.

The cabbie looked in the rear view mirror, and said in his cockney accent, "You got it, gov'nor! I always wanted someone to say that to me!" When they left the curb they also left a little rubber, and a cloud of smoke, as the driver floored it in pursuit of the Mini. "I won't get so close as they'll know we're following 'em, neither!"

"They got to him, too," Nicole spoke softly after Eric ended the call to his handler to let him know his contact was dead. "That's what you don't want to say, isn't it? They have the bones, don't they?" she asked.

The cab threaded its way through London on wide three-laned, tree-lined streets, boasting stately multi-storied buildings erected centuries earlier. The outskirts of the city slowly gave way to two-laned randy shop-lined streets possessing no easements for beautification, and no pretension of grandeur. Now in the seedy district, the cab stopped half a block behind the Mini as it pulled alongside a grimy tenement building.

"They're gettin' out, gov'nor, and they're carryin' somethun," the cabbie stated, watching the events through narrowed eyelids, obviously caught up in the thrilling experience.

"Collins has the box, Eric!"

"He has *a* box. We don't know what's in it for sure. It could be a decoy."

"Your contact is dead, and you still think it could be a decoy? He has the bones, Eric," Nicole said.

"But if they had our box already, Doyle wouldn't have come to us to try to cut a deal."

"So you think it's a double-cross."

"I think they're playing the Chinese buyer against the HHF. Don't forget they're still trying to get what's in the box, too." Eric noticed the cab driver's eyes never made contact with his while the conversation continued in the back seat, even though he was sure the man was curious about what was supposed to be in the box.

As Eric grabbed the fare out of his wallet, the three of them watched Collins and Doyle move cautiously into the tenement building. Eric paid the cabbie without taking his watchful gaze off the actions of Collins and Doyle.

"You Americans are so great! Wait till I tell the wife and kids about this one!"

"We'll make it worth your while to let us sit in your cab while we watch this building," Eric said.

"You American mafia? I don't want no kinda trouble."

"We're the good guys. If you could keep this one to yourself, it would be in the interest of national security, both yours and ours," Eric said to the cabbie.

"Awww, gov'nor! Not even to the wife and kids?"

"Not even to the wife and kids. At least until you're old and gray." Eric peeled off another fifty pounds and passed it over the front seat. "Thanks for your help. Can you pull into that alley so we're not so exposed?" he asked the cabbie.

The cabbie reached back to shake hands with Eric. "Name's Alfred, gov'nor."

Nicole said, "It's probably not safe to enter the building until after dark, unless we have to."

"After dark we'll enter the building, but only if we can do it strategically, meaning we have the upper hand. I don't want either one of us getting killed."

CHAPTER SEVENTEEN

Night had settled into dimly illuminated shadows that stretched down the small alleys between the tall and narrow dreary buildings. Nicole's eyes strained as they watched a very large Hawaiian man, dressed in a cheap Hawaiian print shirt and khaki shorts, exit the front door of the building, dragging a beat-up gray rolling suitcase behind him, one wheel thumping as it rotated on the sidewalk. A tattoo of a skull, and the letters "HHF", were clearly visible on his left arm. As he approached the curb, there was a flash of light inside the building, and the muted, yet unmistakable sound of gunfire.

"We have action," Nicole whispered.

The beefy Hawaiian man stopped at the curb and looked both ways, clearly agitated that his ride was nowhere to be seen.

Just then, a young Asian man appeared across the street, dressed in expensive jeans and a light pink short-sleeved polo shirt, tattoos covering the exposed skin of his arms, creeping up the collar of the shirt to encompass his entire neck before winding their way up the back of his shaved head. In his left hand he clutched a small handgun. He strutted across the road, exuding confidence possessed only by those who had the force of great evil covering their back.

"What the hell?" Eric asked.

Even though they watched the gun as it was raised toward the Hawaiian man, it still stunned all three inside the cab when the shot was fired. The Hawaiian man crumbled to the ground, the hit successfully killing him instantly. The Asian man continued pointing his gun at the dead man, while he casually picked up the handle of the beat-up gray rolling suitcase. A dark blue Jaguar sedan screeched to a halt at the curb where the Asian man gazed with satisfaction at the man lying lifeless on the pavement.

"Bloody hell, gov'nor!"

The Asian man jumped into the back seat of the sedan, dragging the suitcase with him. The sedan peeled away from the curb before the back door was even closed.

A dark green Range Rover raced down the street, slowing just long enough to get a good look a the dead man lying on the sidewalk before speeding away behind the sedan.

"Follow them!" Eric yelled.

The cabbie ran a hand down his face, then shook his head as he fired up the engine. "You got it, gov'nor!"

Eric's heart thumped in his chest as the cabbie, determined to stay with the chase, kept a white-knuckler pace that had him grasping the assist handle on the door of the cab as if his life depended on it. Nicole shot him a look of terror as she grabbed the handle on her side of the cab. Yet despite the speed of the chase through the seamy side of London, the cabbie had enough sense to stay far enough behind so they weren't detected. By the time they left London, Eric thought this might never end. It seemed as if the two cars they were pursuing intended on driving all night to some clandestine destination.

"This is getting expensive, gov'nor," the cabbie said as he looked at Eric in his rearview mirror.

"Just keep following them," Eric said, hoping the chase would end soon.

As they rounded a corner miles from London, a loud popping noise reverberated through the night air. The Range Rover began swerving out of control. The shot fired from the dark blue sedan had been a direct hit to the Rover's driver. When the corner tightened, the dark blue sedan squealed around the tight bend. The Rover flipped end over end.

"Bloody hell!" the cab driver exclaimed.

"The authorities will retrieve it from the ditch once we get a signal and can call it in," Eric said. "Just stay on the blue sedan. Don't let it out of your sight."

"We're getting close to an airfield where I took some parachute classes a couple years ago. I'm guessing that's where they're headed," Nicole said.

Within minutes, the dark blue sedan sped off the road into Headcorn.

"Stay back. Don't let him see us," Eric said to the cab driver.

"Right-o," the driver said, glancing again in the rearview mirror. "Like to tell the wife about this one.

Don't wanna get me-self killed, neither, though, gov'nor."

They watched as the sedan pulled up to what appeared to be a private hangar. The bay doors were wide open. A single-engine turbo prop Pilatus PC-12 idled just in front of the hangar, nose facing the dirt runway with its engine running. Clearly the get-away vehicle.

The Jag screeched to a halt in front of the hanger and the Asian man jumped out of the car, carrying a new Louis Vuitton suitcase. He approached a short, round man, his face drawn taut, as if too many plastic surgeries had left his facial expression suspended in a permanent state of shock. The short man wore a three piece suit and purple silk tie and stood with one foot perched on the step of the passenger door.

"That must be the wealthy Chinese man Doyle mentioned! Eric, we have to stop them! Step on it, Alfred!"

"Get as close to the airplane as you can, Alfred," Eric said.

"Cor blimey, gov'nor! We've got to stop these beastly fellows from stealing what ain't theirs!" The cab squealed as Alfred stomped on the gas pedal.

The young tattooed Chinese man ran toward the airplane, holding the bag out for the older man to grab as Alfred screeched to a halt. He slammed the gear shift into park and jumped out of the cab. Alfred threw himself at the young tattooed Chinese man, knocking him to the ground. Within a half-second, the young Chinese man used a single marshal arts move that sent Alfred flying through the air. He landed on his left side with a loud thump. Alfred groaned, obviously in excruciating pain.

Also trained in marshal arts, Nicole and Eric took on the young Chinese man, limbs flying in full force as the Chinese man tried to overtake them. Finally, pinning the young Chinese man to the ground with her heel against his tattooed throat, Nicole looked up as the wealthy older Chinese man approached her with a small handgun aimed right at her face. Alfred scooted himself quietly toward the cab. The doors still hung open, enabling Alfred to reach inside to the floor and remove a wrench. The Chinese man concentrated on his target, leaving Alfred to go unnoticed as he pulled himself up. The pain that must have been shooting through Alfred's left side had to be excruciating, but he seemed to ignore it as he swung the wrench with full force at the back of the Chinese man's neck. The Chinese man fell to his knees, then toppled over on his right side, his eyes rolling as the lids closed. As the young Chinese man attempted to get up, Eric temporarily immobilized him with one swift move.

Grabbing Nicole and Alfred, Eric said, "Let's get out of here before reinforcements show up! I'm sure that pilot in the airplane has already radioed someone."

Nicole grabbed the Louis Vuitton suitcase and the three of them jumped into the cab.

"Go, go, go!" shouted Eric, pounding on the back of the front seat.

As the cab sped away from the small landing strip, Eric said, "We need to get to Cambridge as soon as possible, Alfred, and since you're in this with us, we'll pay whatever you decide your rate is."

"Even though I feel like a punching bag, not sure I should charge you for all the fun, gov'nor. The wife will never believe this."

"You're a good man, Alfred. Sorry you got hurt," Nicole said.

"Sure, miss, but if I may be so bold as to ask, what is in that suitcase that makes everyone so desperate as to kill over it?"

Eric looked at Nicole. Nicole nodded her head in agreement.

Eric cleared his throat, which suddenly felt parched. "Well, Alfred, what's in the suitcase is something of a national treasure, and we're not really at liberty to discuss it, but just know you have done your country and ours a great service by helping us get the contents of this suitcase where it belongs. The contents of this suitcase are not for sale, at any price. Sadly, though, there will always be people who steal museum pieces. Some quite successfully. But as long as there is breath in me, I am not letting this happen to this particular treasure."

Nicole nodded in agreement, then said, "I thought you didn't want to get killed in the pursuit of the crooks, Alfred. You sure didn't act that way when you tackled that Chinese guy."

Alfred laughed. "Not wanting to be a Nancy boy, I got took over by all the excitement and just wanted to stop these blokes," he said.

"Well, we are very much indebted to you, Alfred," Nicole said. Then she looked at Eric. "I wonder what happened to Collins and Doyle. We never saw them come out of the tenement building."

"I'm sure we'll find out soon enough. My guess is,

though, that their double-crossing got them killed, especially after seeing the HHF guy get shot right out in the open. That tenement building has been vacant for a long time, so I'm sure it was a trap and those two walked straight into it because of greed. The flash of light and the gunshots we heard were probably when the hits went down," Eric said.

"I'm glad we didn't decide to go blasting in there with guns blazing. Obviously, there were more of them than there are of us! Collins and Doyle paid the ultimate price for the treasure they tried to steal," Nicole said.

"We almost lost the treasure too, because it would have disappeared in China. That wealthy Chinese man would have taken those bones out of circulation and they would have never been seen again," Eric said.

"I won't rest until Cook's bones are resting next to his wife," Nicole said. "We're so close now."

Alfred, glanced in his rearview mirror, and said, "Not to speak out of turn, miss, but you mean Captain James Cook, don't ya?"

"You can't breath a word of this, Alfred," Eric said, neither confirming, nor denying Alfred's assumption.

"Don't forget, Eric. We aren't positive of what's inside the suitcase yet," Nicole said.

CHAPTER EIGHTEEN

Inside the suitcase, the box containing the bones had been strapped to the side of the suitcase. Eric removed it and then opened it. The bones were inside. He began accounting for each one aloud, ensuring they still had all the bones that were in the basket when they'd removed them from the cave. The smallish skull with the wide forehead and high cheekbones still intact, and the silver medal were all there, confirming these were indeed Cook's bones.

"Everything is here," he said, rewrapping the package and placing it back inside the basket that had originally contained them. "We'll keep it in the box for transport to the church."

"So what now?" she asked, probably more confident than ever that she would fulfill her promise.

"I've made arrangements to visit the church. But you have to prepare yourself for the fact that it might be impossible to put the bones into the same grave as Cook's wife and son."

"What do you mean? I promised Gran."

"I realize that, babe," he said, tucking a stray lock of blonde hair behind her left ear. "But it might not work out that way. It depends on several factors."

Her eyes narrowed, fire glinting in her steady gaze. "You're not using this to get the bones back to some musty hole in the States are you?"

"Cor, gov'ner, you're not are ya?" Alfred asked, his eyes wide as he glanced at Eric in the rear view mirror.

Eric's hand dropped. The frustration that swept across his mind was just shy of anger. He turned away from her. He couldn't let her see the annoyance in his face at her overt accusation.

"Are you?" In his current frame of mind, her tone sounded like the hairy edge of hysteria.

"I assure you, I am doing nothing of the kind." The edge in his voice was intended to help her regain her composure, but even to him, it reverberated anger. And he didn't want her to know just how deep she'd just driven the stake of distrust.

She clamped a delicate hand on his shoulder and said, "Hey, lighten up! I'm kidding." Gentle laughter rippled through the small room. "If you were going to double-cross me you'd have already done it."

"It certainly didn't sound like kidding." To have his integrity questioned was unacceptable. Especially since he'd risked his neck more than once for this woman. "Once we get the bones buried we can walk away from each other. No strings attached. I held up my end of the bargain," he said with anger he couldn't keep at bay any longer.

"She's kidding, gov'nor," Alfred chimed in, distress now etching his soft face.

The furrow between Nicole's brow suggested confusion. But in his mind there was nothing to be confused about. Even if she said she was kidding, it was evident that she still had a great deal of doubt about him.

Which meant the foundation of their relationship had a crack in it as wide as Waimea Canyon.

"I'm sorry. You thought I was serious, but I really *was* just kidding," she said, sliding her hand down his back before he stepped away from her. "Why does it seem like I'm always apologizing to you?"

Compartmentalizing his feelings, He picked up the basket. "Like you said, Alfred. She was just kidding." He turned to Nicole. "Forget it. Let's head to Cambridge."

During the long ride in Alfred's cab, first back through London traffic then on into the countryside, by the time they parked in front of the church, Nicole somehow had managed to begin convincing him she trusted him, and that she really had been joking. He knew it was hard for her to believe in someone. And no one understood that more than him. So he resolved to accept things at face value, his resistance collapsing at the thought of walking away from her once the bones were buried, like he had been forced to when he'd ended their engagement a few years ago. Besides, he couldn't sit this close to her and keep his hands to himself. With her face turned toward him as she prattled on and on, he impulsively placed his left hand on the back of her head and pressed his mouth over hers. The kiss was like a soldering iron joining two metals.

Her response filled him with relief. If her searching

hands and soft moans meant anything, he should accept her apology. He'd been accused of being overly-sensitive about his integrity by someone else who had the power to destroy him years ago, but now he decided it was unfair to hold the woman he loved hostage for that incident.

When she pulled her face away from his, tears glistened in her eyes. "Forgive me for not trusting you?"

He leaned his forehead against hers and closed his eyes. "How can I not? You mean the world to me."

"Then why did you say we should go our separate ways?" she asked, her eyes still watery.

"I almost ended up in jail because someone in the CIA questioned my integrity. It's a hot button for me. And if you're honest with yourself you'll admit you didn't trust me at all in the beginning."

"With the exception of Gran, I can't say I've been able to trust anyone. And she's gone now. When that plane crashed in Africa, I stopped trusting even myself. It isn't something that comes easy to me," she said, rubbing her forehead as if it would dissolve the memories.

"But when you love someone you have to trust them. Same goes for me too, babe," he added, his penetrating gaze extracting everything she had to give.

"How...do you --"

"Know you love me?" His smile radiated his feelings. "You said so two nights ago." He ran a long well-groomed finger down her pert nose. "When you thought I was asleep."

"And do you trust me?" she asked.

"Are you fishing for a declaration?"

"Not if you're not swimming in the stream."

"And if I am?"

"Then I'm fishing."

His mouth swept down over hers again leaving her no doubt as to his emotions. "Satisfied?"

"Why, yes, sir, I am! Indeed I am!" Alfred said, then chuckled.

Nicole looked from Alfred to Eric. "As usual, you're making me work for what I want."

A sensual smile spread across Eric's lips. "I love you, Nikki. I've never stopped loving you since the day I carried you out of the wreckage in Africa. Are you satisfied?"

"But --"

"No buts."

"And do you trust me?" she asked, merriment twinkling in her beautiful blue eyes.

"Enough to let you save my life," he said. "Now let's see if we can get rid of the contents of this basket to your satisfaction."

"Mind if I join you when we get there, love?" Alfred's gaze locked with Nicole's.

"I think you deserve it," she said as Eric's head dipped in agreement.

It seemed Eric had more contacts than just the dead man they'd left in the bathroom at the pub, because someone had gotten to the vicar ahead of them. Whatever they did, when they arrived at Elizabeth Cook's grave in the middle aisle of the church, it already lay open, waiting for Captain Cook to finally be reunited with his wife. The vicar of St. Andrew the Great at Cambridge also awaited their arrival. Both Nicole and Eric examined the opening. A tribute to the bodies buried there was engraved on a plain stone sarcophagus. Eric squatted on his right heel and gently placed the basket beside the sarcophagus. The vicar said a prayer then made the sign of the cross over the grave. If Captain Cook's Elizabeth had been alive to share this moment, it would have made Elizabeth's grieving less wretched when her husband died. At least that's what the romantic in Nicole believed.

Once the ceremony ended, the vicar waved his hand and a stocky man in coveralls appeared from the shadows and began resetting the flagstones.

"'Tis a solemn moment, gov'nor," Alfred said in reverence.

"Do you mind if we take a look around, Eric? Gran told me there are inscriptions on the walls. I'd like to read them," Nicole whispered. "You're welcome to join us, Alfred."

"Wouldn't miss it for the world, love."

"I believe what you wish to see is on the north wall of the sanctuary miss," said the vicar in low tones as he nodded in the direction of the north wall.

Eric took Nicole's hand in his as they approached the inscriptions.

They stood, hands clasped, Eric's thumb caressing hers as they read the lengthy commemoration of Captain James Cook. At the end Nicole traced the carved inscription with the tip of her right forefinger.

"It's amazing, Eric. After supposedly being buried at sea in 1779, but in reality hidden away all these years in a cave, Captain James Cook has finally been laid to rest next to his wife."

"Imagine what he might have accomplished had he

not met such an untimely death at fifty-one. It is said he was one of the greatest Englishmen to ever live. He accomplished amazing things during his short lifetime."

"And his poor wife," she whispered. "While he was at sea, she buried three children, two just months old, and the other only four years old." Alfred tisk-tisked at her elbow as he shook his head.

"She must have had high hopes for their other children, but they all died young too," Eric said. "The youngest and the oldest died thirty-two days apart."

"I wouldn't be able to go on if I were her."

Eric shook his head. "Elizabeth died at ninety-three, outliving all of her children by forty-one years. According to history, Captain Cook's death was a blow to both the English *and* the Hawaiians. I'm just glad he had a sister to carry on the family lineage because that means I am his great-niece."

"With several greats between you, love," Alfred added.

Her upturned face reflected both sadness and relief. "I'm just glad we finally got his bones where they should have been taken in 1779, instead of being paraded around the islands as a trophy." She paused for a moment. "But I wonder why no one tried to stop us from bringing them here. Are we delusional, or have we outsmarted everyone else?"

"Since we got the bones in the grave, and that guy back there is cementing them in, it's safe to assume we're not delusional." He put his arms around her in a loose embrace. "Have I told you how amazing you are?"

She beamed up at him, love shining through her

eyes. "Not today."

"Well, you are. Now how about that sunset date on the beach?" he asked.

Eric turned toward Alfred and asked, "Willing to drive us, Alfred?"

"Cor blimey, gov'nor," Alfred said as a blush spread from his neck to his soft face. "I'd be honored. But what beach ya talking 'bout? And can I tell the wife?"

THE END

Made in the USA
San Bernardino, CA
16 August 2015